RON BASE
MAIN STREET
MILTON

RON BASE
MAIN STREET MILTON

West-End Books

Library and Archives Canada Cataloguing in Publication data is available upon request.
978-0-9940645-7-8

Publisher's Note: This is a work of fiction. Names, characters, places, and incidents either are products of the author's imagination or are used fictitiously. Any resemblance to actual persons, events, or locales is entirely coincidental.

Printed and bound in Canada

West-End Books
133 Mill St.
Milton, Ontario
L9T 1S1

Cover design and co-ordination: Jennifer Smith
Text design and electronic formatting: Ric Base
Author photograph: Doug Mohun
Cover photo: Adam Smith

First Edition

If you want a happy ending, that depends, of course, on where you stop the story.

-Orson Welles

Readers should know there is a real place called Milton. From Toronto, you drive west an hour or so (depending on traffic), turn south on Highway 25, and soon you have reached the town. That's the real Milton. The Milton you will experience in these pages, while accurate insofar as setting, is, nonetheless, a fictional Milton, the Milton out of this author's slightly diabolical imagination.

1

There was a hanging man.

Visible through early morning mist, hanging from a lamppost on Main Street, Milton.

The hanging man on a street dating from the 1800s, its old brick buildings exhausted from the fight for survival in an age demanding constant expansion with less and less use for landmarks. A street of broken dreams you could say, business after business coming and going, a street now of Italian restaurants and barber shops, struggling.

Not helped this mist-filled morning by the sight of the man hanging from a lamppost.

He was discovered by Angus McDonald at 6:15 a.m. Angus was out for his morning walk following a triple heart bypass.

Having ascertained the identity of the hanging man, he calmly called 911. "The mayor is hanging from a lamppost on Main Street," Angus said.

"What?" demanded the 911 operator.

"You heard me," Angus said. "The mayor. Jock Whitlock."

"I know who the mayor is," the 911 operator said peevishly.

"Yeah well he's hanging from a light post."

"What's his condition?" asked the 911 operator regaining her professional demeanor.

"His condition is he's dead," Angus said.

Officers responded five minutes later, parking near the bench where Angus waited.

"Jesus Christ, it is the goddamn mayor," said officer Todd Bristol, who had been with the Halton force for ten years.

"That's what I've been trying to get through a lot of thick skulls this morning," said Angus from his seat on the bench.

Bristol's partner, Danny Grady, with the force only three years, stood still, hands on his hips, shaking his head, saying, "Goddamn."

Officer Bristol pulled himself together, realizing this was a shitstorm unfolding, thus the sooner the higher-ups were here, the better. He radioed the duty sergeant and told him what had happened and maybe someone should get in touch with the chief.

Meanwhile, Danny Grady had his notebook out and was questioning Angus McDonald about what he had seen and when he saw it.

A couple of joggers wearing Nike shorts appeared and stopped, mouths agape at the sight of the town's mayor.

More police arrived including the duty sergeant who ordered officers to cordon off the street and push what was becoming a growing crowd—where did these people come from this early in the morning? —back out of sight around the corner.

The sergeant radioed for even more officers, along with Glen Petrusiak and Mickey Dann, the two detectives who happened to be on duty that morning.

It took them the better part of an hour to get there. When Mickey came onto the street, he stopped and looked up at the body in disbelief. "Jesus Christ," he said quietly as Petrusiak joined him.

"One hell of a way to take yourself out," Petrusiak said.

Mickey gave his partner a sidewise glance. "What are you talking about?"

"This is suicide, right?"

Mickey spent some time looking at the body.

"It is suicide." Petrusiak pronounced, no longer asking a question.

"What the hell," Mickey said.

———————

The telephone call woke Jean Whitlock from a sound sleep.

She had spent the day arranging furniture in the living room of the two-story frame heritage home she had recently purchased, overseeing the painters putting the finishing touches to the C2 cornbread yellow walls in the kitchen, giving too much attention to a silent debate over whether the pattern of the blue Moroccan cactus silk carpet did or did not fight with the blue encaustic tiled floor in the ensuite bathroom. Consuming stuff that kept her mind off everything else in her life. Everything that she didn't want to think about; everything much less important than the question of the cactus silk carpet and the blue encaustic tiled bathroom floor.

Until the phone rang.

Groggily, she reached for the cell phone on the floor beside her bed. The screen said Mickey Dann was calling. Well, well, she thought, it was about time. She had not heard from him in weeks, wondered if she would ever hear from him. Wondered if she cared one way or the other. "This is a surprise," Jean said.

"Sorry to bother you this early in the morning," Mickey said.

"What's up?"

"I want you to meet me on Main Street," Mickey said.

"Right now?"

"As soon as you can get here."

"I don't understand," Jean said, hearing the tightness in Mickey's voice. "What's going on?"

"Do me a favor will you? Just get over here."

The line went dead.

She got out of bed, the kind of cold fear running through her body she never wanted to experience again, suspecting that soon the clash of the Moroccan cactus carpet with the bathroom tile wasn't going to matter a damn.

By the time Jean got through the police lines holding back curious onlookers and reached Main Street, Irwin "Doc" Prescott the district medical examiner had arrived and, along with everyone else, stood gawking at the hanging corpse.

Jean let out an involuntary gasp when she saw that it was her uncle. Doc spotted her and came over and embraced her. "Jesus H. Christ," he said.

She had known Doc Prescott forever, but even so she didn't want him embracing her, didn't want anyone touching her right now. His breath was stale first thing in the morning. She eased herself away as Doc Prescott said, "This is so terrible, Jean. Who would have thought it would have come to this?"

Except what had it come to? Jean wondered. Mickey Dann, looking grim, loomed behind her. She said, "Mickey."

"A passerby found him like this," he said.

Jean thought dully, Who else would find him?

She forced herself to approach the body. The morning breeze blew at Jock's unkempt hair. His chin was covered in a gray stubble matching the gray business suit that went nicely with the collarless white shirt. His fine, patrician head was at an angle, eyes wide open, bulging slightly. Not a happy death, thought Jean. But then, she silently concluded, staring numbly, you wouldn't expect a man hanging from a lamppost to have died happy.

Would you?

Mickey came and stood beside her. "It is the mayor?"

Jean looked at him.

Mickey shrugged. "I have to ask."

Jean swallowed back hard the choking in her throat. "It's Jock."

"Your uncle."

"Yes," Jean said.

Mickey asked, "Any idea how this happened?"

Jean shook her head.

"We're thinking suicide," Mickey said.

Jean didn't say anything. Doc Prescott joined them. Mickey said, "You agree, Doc?"

"Don't know anything yet," he said.

Mickey pressed: "What else could it be?"

Doc shrugged. "Jock going out with some flare rather than face going on trial in a couple of days for the murder of his wife? Possible. Anything's possible at this point. We'll see."

"Let me ask you this," Jean said, keeping her eyes on her uncle. "how do you suppose he got up there in the first place?"

Mickey and Doc Prescott stared up at the body. Neither man spoke.

"I mean there's nothing underneath him," Jean went on. "If he did this alone, if he killed himself, how did he get up there?"

2

Jock Whitlock had been the larger-than-life mayor of Milton for as long as Jean could remember.

As a little girl, she always looked forward to visiting him at his spacious Old Town Hall corner office. Even when she showed up unexpectedly, he found time for her. Later, as a teenager, he arranged to have lunch with her at Victoria Park in front of the Town Hall, seated on a bench eating the tuna sandwiches the mayor always brought along.

In those years, she came to regard him as a mentor, the calm voice in her life when the cacophony of her family became unbearable, particularly after she let it be known that she had decided to join the Royal Canadian Mounted Police. After all, the Whitlock Family for generations had buried Milton's dead. Jean had already trained as an undertaker. Why would she ever want to become a police woman? Where did that come from?

While everyone else derided her decision, Jock quietly counseled her to follow her own instincts. That's what counted in the end, not the wishes of her family.

It was only after she joined the Force and gained experience in the deceitful ways of the world that Jean began to suspect her beloved uncle was not quite what he had always seemed to her.

Jock wore two faces, she learned: the loving uncle who seemingly would do anything for her, and the smart, crafty politician with only a light grasp on qualities such as honesty and morality; a man willing to do what needed to be done in order to achieve his goals and at the same time line his pockets.

The more she became suspicious of Jock, the harder he tried to retain her belief in him, particularly after she left the Force in disgrace and moved back to Milton. She might have bought into his efforts had Jock's young wife, Desiree, not been found murdered in her car.

Did Jock kill her? That's what his trial was supposed to ascertain. Now it would never happen and there was a new question in the air: Did Mayor Jock Whitlock, unwilling to face the indignity of a trial, take his own life?

Or was he murdered?

Jock lay inviting an answer to that question under a bright light on a metal table inside the Halton morgue, a white sheet pulled up to his chest. The answer was not immediately forthcoming, Jean thought, as she gazed at his corpse, bone white beneath the hard light, his face in repose relieved of the stress of living. She would not take her eyes off him, not for a while as she tried to summon any kind of emotion—unable to do it.

"Jean." Doc Prescott's voice came from behind, drawing her out of her reverie. "What do you think, Doc?" she asked only because there didn't seem to be anything else to ask.

Doc Prescott merely shrugged non-committally. "Like I keep saying, yet to be determined."

"You've been at this since I was a kid," Jean said. "You must have a sense."

"Well, you have to say the circumstances looks suspicious." Doc was choosing his words with uncharacteristic care.

"Like how he managed to hang himself from a lamppost?"

"That's a consideration, certainly. Also, there were small amounts of suspicious-looking dirt and grass strains on his trousers and on the elbows of his jacket. What does that mean? Was he killed somewhere else and then moved onto Main Street? Or did he slip on his lawn on the way to his car?"

"Which was found in the parking lot across from James Street."

"Exactly," Doc said. "If someone killed him, they drove Jock to Main Street and then hung him from the lamppost."

"What about time of death? Does that tell you anything?"

"Using the rule of thumb that a body cools about two degrees in the first hour after death, and then one degree in the hours after that, I'm estimating he died sometime around five o'clock in the morning."

"He was found at six thirty. Plenty of time to kill Jock somewhere else and then move the body."

"Contrarily," Doc said, "given the time of the morning, he could just as easily have hung there for that time period before anyone found him."

"No other indications of how he might have died?"

"No gunshot or stab wounds, if that's what you mean. Was he drugged? My autopsy should tell me more. Strangulation is the obvious possibility, but then the question becomes when was he strangled? The nylon rope around his neck could have been used to do the job before he arrived at the lamppost. We'll see."

"Knowing how Jock liked to grandstand, it might not be any more complicated than he killed himself," Jean said.

"There is that possibility, definitely," Doc agreed. "For the moment, however, Mickey Dann is treating this as a suspicious death. If that's the case then I imagine the question he will be asking himself is who would want to murder our beloved mayor?"

"Not so beloved," Jean said. "Given what Jock was up to, the list could be long."

"Almost certainly," Doc agreed. "But then you've got to wonder who would kill him and then go to the trouble—and take the risk—of hanging him in plain sight on Main Street?"

"To make a statement?"

"What kind of statement would the killer want to make?"

Doc's question hung in the air, unanswerable. Jean looked at her uncle on a cold metal table thinking, this is how the great Jock Whitlock has ended up. Naked and dead. Under a bright, unforgiving light.

3

That unanswered question was on many lips at the memorial service for Jock after the medical examiner had completed the autopsy and the police had released the body.

Jean found herself in the peculiar position of planning the service with help from Doris Stamper, who had bought the funeral business from Jean after the death of her brother, Bryce. Jock was yet another sad twist in the ongoing tragedy dogging the Whitlock family these past few years.

To her dismay, there was an impressive turnout inside the faded elegance of the Whitlock Funeral Home. The locals showed up, most of them elderly, well served by Jock over the years. Whatever else he did, Jock always made sure he took care of his constituents. On the day of his farewell, they came dutifully to say goodbye.

Members of Milton's town council made an appearance despite the disgrace their mayor had brought on them and the town. Their presence was not unexpected, Jean supposed, even if they were noticeably uncomfortable, sitting together, making small talk, shifting around in the chairs set up for them at the front near the lectern.

The police chief, Walt Dunnell, was there, too, a big, blustery guy swaggering in his dress blues. He was accompanied by Mickey Dann and Glen Petrusiak, the detectives charged with investigating Jock's suspicious death.

The last person whose presence Jean expected was Ontario's premier, Eve Harriot. She recalled that Eve Harriot and Jock had known each other for more than two decades, from the time Jock ran unsuccessfully in a provincial election. It was one of the few times a Conservative had failed to get elected in the area. Eve knew a useful ally when she met one and thus had remained in touch with Jock, not friends exactly, two political animals learning to survive in the jungle. One political animal did not desert another simply because one of them was charged with murder and ended up hanging from a lamppost, Jean mused, as she moved to introduce herself to the premier.

"Yes, you're the Mountie, are you not?" Eve said, inspecting Jean with her trademark cool gaze, the one her critics claimed she wore like a mask so that it was impossible to see what Eve Harriot was thinking. That is, her critics often added, if she was thinking anything at all beyond winning the next election.

"I used to be," Jean said.

"You caused quite a fuss when you left if I recall correctly. Jock spoke admiringly of you many times." Jean half expected her to add, "until recently." But the words were only suggested.

As usual, the fifty-five-year-old premier wore red—a red blazer this morning. Eve always wore red and therefore had been dubbed the Red Queen by a less-than-adoring Toronto press. The Red Queen was an avid hunter, a passion that had led two years before to the death of her husband, Ed. An accident, the mourning Red Queen said, mistaking Ed for a deer. A coroner's jury had debated thirty minutes before exonerating the premier. The people forgave her trespass, too, and returned her and her party to office less than a year later.

Even now, she remained popular given the rough and tumble of provincial politics. She was a tough, pragmatic woman, skilled in the art of political street-fighting who, in addition to accidentally killing her husband, had managed to duck and weave around scandals that would have brought down a lesser politician. But the Red Queen endured in the face of many adversities. You messed with her at your peril.

Eve was joined by a slim young Asian woman wearing glasses and an eager smile. She introduced herself: "Amy Wu-Chan. I'm the premier's executive assistant." She spoke with an eagerness that matched her smile. "So sorry about your uncle."

There was more to Amy than her role as "executive assistant" Jean—and just about everyone else—had heard. Since her husband's death, rumors swirled—did rumors do anything else? —that Eve and Amy had become a couple. Nothing was said officially but increasingly it was a given that they were together.

"Amy was wonderful helping me get through my husband's death," Eve added, as though Amy might be able to serve in the same capacity for Jean.

"Is that so?" replied Jean, non-committally.

"Times like this, you need a friend," said Amy, the eagerness dialed down to heartfelt understanding.

Before Jean was forced to come up with an answer to that particular observation, Eve was distracted by a passing familiar face and was off to shake a hand, leaving her alone with Amy. The heartfelt smile evaporated. Amy was all business. "The premier would like to talk to you," she said.

Jean looked at her, not sure what to say.

"After the service," Amy added.

"She wants to talk to me?"

"In private, if that's all right with you."

"Yes," was all Jean could manage.

"Good. I'll come and get you when it's over."

Then, she too, was gone, leaving Jean alone but not for long. A voice said, "Jean Whitlock?"

She turned to find herself face to face with a tall man with piercing eyes and an impressively jutting jaw. A dazzler, she thought in the instant before she could properly edit herself and not think like that.

"Peter Earp," he said, extending a hand.

She took his hand and said, "Yes," as though she had some idea who Peter Earp was when, in truth, she had no idea.

"I'm the new guy at Caulder International."

In other words, with Del Caulder behind bars, Peter Earp, the rather enigmatic Toronto-based entrepreneur almost overnight had become the province's biggest developer.

Jean said, "You mean you're the guy who bought out Del."

"With a good deal of help and guidance from your uncle, I should say," Peter Earp said.

Jean immediately wondered what kind of "help and guidance" Jock might have brought to that particular party.

"I'm sorry for what's happened," Peter continued. "I wanted to be here to pay my respects."

"Thank you," Jean said.

"I'm new in town, trying to get around a bit, meet people. Your uncle always spoke highly of you."

Apparently, Jock had spent a lot of time speaking highly of her. When he wasn't busy lining his own pockets, killing his wife, or getting himself hanged on a lamppost in downtown Milton.

Good old Jock, she thought.

"I'd like to get together at some point," Peter went on. "Have a chat. If your free that is."

"I'm not sure what we would chat about," Jean said.

"Like I say, I'm trying to get my bearings here. You know this town, you could be a great help."

"I see in *The Champion* where you're trying to get approval for a townhouse development at the fairgrounds."

"That's the plan, yes."

"You know Mr. Earp, I've spent a great deal of my life here and I still don't know this town at all. So good luck."

Peter just grinned and shook her hand. "We'll see each other again, Ms. Whitlock."

"Will we?"

"I'm sure of it," he said.

4

The afternoon passed in a blur for Jean.

The blur intermittently took on human form. The premier, for instance, was astute enough not to be on record about any lingering feelings she might have had for Jock Whitlock, and so she did not participate in the eulogies. Jean also stayed quiet. Anything she would say about her uncle at this point, she decided, should not be said at a funeral.

Amar Bal, a Sikh with an extraordinarily full beard and an engagingly gentle manner, Milton's deputy mayor and therefore, for the moment, acting mayor, delivered a carefully worded eulogy. He outlined how Jock had presided over the transformation of Milton from a sleepy farming community into the fastest growing town in Canada, avoiding any suggestion of Jock's corruption or mention of the murder of Jock's wife.

Bal ended with a plea for unity "in this time of uncertainty. The people of Milton are strong, proud of their history and diversity, they stick together no matter what. This is what we must do now. We must be together. We must be strong." He then raised his fist and began to call out, "Milton strong! Milton strong! Milton strong!"

No one joined in the chant. Everyone looked uneasy. A stony silence descended as Bal fled the podium.

Grace Travis, Jock's longtime, longsuffering secretary, the woman he was always going to marry even as he married someone else, provided what little emotion anyone could summon. A sparrow-like woman, not unattractive but, everyone agreed, certainly not the sort of woman Jock tended to marry, Grace strode to the front carrying a sheaf of papers which she spread out on the lectern. She then spent several moments reviewing them before she announced with a breaking voice how much she had loved Jock Whitlock.

"I knew he wasn't perfect. I saw firsthand his imperfections, but that didn't matter. I loved him anyway," she said. "You should know that. You should know how much I loved him, no matter what."

And that was it. Grace rushed from the room, leaving more uneasy silence. That pretty much broke up the memorial. There was nothing else to say. Nothing good anyway. And if there was, no one could think of it, least of all Jean. She just wanted out of there.

The sun at two o'clock in the afternoon was hot and bright, the beauty of the day failing to acknowledge the passing of one of Milton's tarnished sons. Jean stood taking deep, resuscitative breaths. The usual knot of smokers gathered further along the walkway eyed her surreptitiously as they drew deeply on their cigarettes. Mickey Dann came out and stood beside her. "Don't ask me if I'm all right," Jean said.

"Never crossed my mind," Mickey said. "As long as you don't ask me how I'm doing."

"I guessed you are doing fine since I never hear from you," Jean replied.

"You could call me," Mickey said.

"I could," Jean said.

"But?"

"Then I would end up questioning you about the investigation of my uncle's death, and you wouldn't like that."

"No, I wouldn't," Mickey said agreeably.

"So, I'm not going to ask you."

"Good."

"Even though I could probably help."

"Could you?"

"I don't know."

"There you go," Mickey said. "Right back to it's a good thing you didn't ask me."

"The story of our lives," Jean said. "Running around in circles."

"You can't even remember dating me in high school."

"That's not true," she said. "I *vaguely* remember dating you."

"Then we're making progress."

Jean missed the arrival of Amy Wu-Chan until Mickey nodded slightly and Jean turned to see Amy beside her, professionally bright smile in place. "Sorry to interrupt," she said. "The premier would like that word with you, Jean, if you have time for her."

Jean gave Amy a mystified look before she said, "Where is the premier?"

"She's waiting in the car," Amy said.

5

A familiar face stood guard at the side of the premier's black Cadillac Escalade.

Pierre Dorval's hair had turned white since the last time Jean saw him and a dark blue business suit had replaced his Mounted Police uniform. But Pierre, with his wiry muscular frame, continued to display the results of a rigorous daily workout. His face maintained the combination of accommodation and danger that had helped propel his career over the years although Jean had a vague recollection that he had left the Force under a cloud. But then she was hardly one to talk about clouds.

"Hello, Jean," Pierre said in the gravelly voice touched with the accent that betrayed his Quebecois roots. The smile on his face as she approached was pleasant enough. "Do you remember me?"

"Pierre. It's been a while."

"It has," Pierre agreed. "I hope you are well."

Amy Wu-Chan walking a few steps behind Jean said, "You two know each other?"

"We served together," Jean said.

"Yes. I forget Pierre was a Mountie. Well, now he is the premier's personal bodyguard. He's moved up in the world. Isn't that right, Pierre?"

Pierre blessed the question with a weak smile. "Anything you say, Ms. Wu-Chan."

"That's right, Pierre. Anything I say."

The smile disappeared as Pierre opened the back-passenger door. Jean gave Amy a sidewise glance. "It's all right. "I'll wait out here with my friend, Pierre."

Pierre's expression was frozen as Jean climbed into the back. Eve Harriot seemed to overwhelm her space. Jean felt as though she had to huddle in a corner in order to give the Red Queen enough room. The door closed. The interior fell into gloom, Eve in enough shadow to obscure any friendliness that might otherwise have been contained in her smile. Or maybe, Jean thought, there was none to begin with.

"Thanks for this, Jean," Eve said.

"Certainly," was all Jean could think to say, unsure exactly what she was being thanked for.

"I know this has been a difficult day for you—a difficult time, I imagine. I don't want to make it any more difficult than it already is."

Jean remained silent, waiting to hear how the premier of the province could make her time more difficult.

"I'm not sure if you know, but Jock and I go back a long way," Eve went on. "Many years together in the trenches of local politics. I was just a kid from Thunder Bay. What did I know? But Jock knew, and he imparted a few lessons. Not only in politics but in the realities of life."

Jean thought of the lessons she thought Jock had provided over the years; a lot of lies as it turned out.

"As a matter of fact," the premier went on. "Jock introduced me to my husband, Ed."

"I didn't know that," Jean said. And Jock had never said anything.

"Ed was a mover and shaker if there ever was one. A rainmaker who loved to make the rain. He had great plans for Jock but, in the end, Jock was content to stay in local politics. I had bigger ambitions. Not loftier, just a little bigger, that's all." She paused as though to either consider the past or gather her thoughts as to what she would say next. Jean couldn't tell which.

"That brings us, sadly, to where we are today; the unfolding tragedy of Jock Whitlock finally at an end." Another pause before Eve said, "Except it isn't at an end. I'm afraid Jock's death presents difficulties that none of us could have imagined."

"Does it?" Jean interjected.

In shadow, Jean could see the Red Queen's mouth stiffen. "I think you'll agree that Jock has caused everyone more than enough problems. The scandals, the murder charges, the way he ended his life—"

"Is that what he did?" Jean couldn't stop herself interrupting the premier. "You believe *he* ended his life?"

Eve looked vaguely surprised. "Are we supposed to think he didn't?"

"I don't know," Jean said. "The medical examiner has yet to determine the cause of death. For the moment, nobody is thinking much of anything."

Eve shifted around as though searching for her lost train of thought. "Then my point is reinforced. Jock creating more headlines, even in death. I'd like it to stop."

"I'm not sure even the premier of the province can make that happen," Jean said dryly.

In the dimness, the Red Queen's smile made a brief reappearance. "Yes, I'm afraid you may be right, Jean. However, I believe Jock named you as the executor of his estate. Am I correct about that?"

Now it was Jean's turn to show surprise. "How would you know, Madam Premier?"

"Let's say it's my job to know what I need to know," she said. "You are the executor, are you not?"

"To my surprise, yes."

"You will be going through Jock's files, I assume, getting his papers in order, that sort of thing."

"I suppose I will have to do that, why?"

"I'd like you to do me a favor, Jean. I don't think you will find anything of a compromising nature, anything pertaining to the relationship I had with Jock. But if you should come across something, before you do anything, I'd like you to get in touch with me. Can I ask you to do that?"

Jean hesitated before she said, "I guess my question would be something along the lines of, what am I liable to find?"

A flash of irritation crossed the Red Queen's face. "As I stated before," she said carefully, "I don't think you will find anything. I don't have specifics but if there is—"

"If I come across something, I will at least let you know about it," Jean said, choosing her words with the same care as the premier. "I can't promise you much more than that."

"You can't? Or you won't?"

"I'll do what I can," Jean said non-committally.

Eve did not seem to fill the car so much. Her obvious concern about what Jock Whitlock in death might be able to do had diminished her, reduced her in Jean's eyes to another worried suspect, the kind she had encountered many times over her years with the Mounties. She felt on more solid ground now; this was a person she could handle.

"I'm not asking you to do anything that you shouldn't do, Jean," the premier continued. "But let's stay in touch. No matter how this plays out, you're an impressive woman and now, more than ever, I need impressive women around me."

Eve passed Jean a card. "My personal cell phone number. Call me any time. There are a lot of things we can do together. Let's not waste any time. Let's get started."

Jean took the card. Once again, the Red Queen filled the car. She had regained control. As if by prearranged magic, the door opened and the shine of Amy Wu-Chan's face lit the interior. "We're running a little late, Madam Premier," Amy said brightly.

Eve reached out and squeezed Jean's hand. "Thank you, Jean. I look forward to hearing from you soon."

6

What had she agreed to? Jean wondered once she got home, got out of her funeral garb and into sweats, mulling over her encounter with Premier Eve Harriot as she poured herself a glass of wine.

The workmen had left for the day. The house smelled of fresh paint. Out with the old. In with the new. A fresh start.

Right.

Glass in hand, she wandered upstairs to inspect the cactus silk carpet with narrowing eyes. Did it clash with the bathroom tile or not? A little bit, maybe. But she loved the rug. And the floor tile. She would learn to live with both.

Back downstairs, inspecting yet again the new sofa and chairs. Had she made the right choice? And had she agreed to something with Eve Harriot? Or, more accurately, that the Red Queen believed she had agreed. What? To alert the province's premier to anything incriminating that Jock might have hidden away? The duplicitous, shape-shifting Jock, the moment you thought you knew him, concluded that he could no longer fool you with another jaw-dropping revelation, up popped the Red Queen to erase any such suppositions.

If there was something what was it? And where was it hidden away?

Somewhere in the dark nooks and crannies of his life? The mind roiled with possibility. Jock had spent a lifetime dealing from the bottom of the deck. Illegal kickbacks from Del Caulder and the murder of his wife might not be the end of it.

Enter the Red Queen, clearly worried about what her old friend might have left up his sleeve for Jean to find. Now the question was, what would she do if she found it?

She did not have the answer.

Yet.

Her cell phone began to vibrate on the counter. She wasn't going to answer until she saw the name on the readout. The office of the mayor. Well, it wouldn't be Uncle Jock that much was certain.

"Hello, Grace," Jean said when she swiped the phone open. "I didn't think you'd still be at the office."

"I came back after the funeral to wrap up a few things," Grace Travis said in that gentle, unchallenging voice Jean had heard so many times over the years calling to summon her to lunch with her uncle. Jean always thought Grace should be reading children's stories to a kindergarten class. The kids would love her as everyone loved her. Everyone except Jock, that is. The one person in the world she wanted to love and he never loved her back. He said he did, but he didn't.

But then, Jean long ago surmised, Jock never loved anyone. Not even himself.

"We didn't have a chance to talk this afternoon," Grace went on. "I was too overwhelmed. I had to get out of there."

"I understand," Jean said. "I don't think any of us wanted to be there longer than necessary."

"I couldn't be around those people who all hated him and yet were there supposedly to honor him. It was so terribly hypocritical."

"Yes, I suppose it was," Jean said, thinking she was one of those people, although maybe hate was too strong a word for how she felt. Conflicted fit better.

"I understand from the lawyers that you are Jock's executor," she said in a strained voice.

"I'm sorry, Grace," Jean said. "It should have been you. I don't know what Jock was thinking."

"You're his closest living relative," Grace said. "It just makes sense. Besides, what difference does it make?" Grace said this in a way that suggested it made a great deal of difference.

"I'm still going to need your help," Jean said.

"There are a lot of files. As soon as I heard what happened, I gathered together everything in his office."

"Yes, that's helpful," Jean said.

"I knew the police would come. I didn't want them poking around until you had a chance to look at them."

"When Jock was arrested for murder, did they not go through everything?"

"Not everything," Jean said.

"Where are the files now?"

"In the trunk of my car," Grace said. "A dozen boxes."

"A dozen boxes?" Jean groaned inwardly.

"Can I bring them around?"

"When do you want to do this?"

"Right now," Grace said. "The sooner you have them, the better."

"What do you think, Grace?"

"What do I think about what?" Grace, gently evasive.

"Do you think Jock killed himself?"

Silence on the other end of the phone. Then Grace said, "I believe Jock was sick and tired of everything. He was probably going to go to jail for the rest of his life. He couldn't face that humiliation."

"So he hanged himself on a lamppost on Main Street?"

"I don't think there is any other reasonable explanation, do you?"

"I don't know," Jean said with an honesty that surprised her. "Hanging himself from a lamppost doesn't seem like much of a reasonable explanation. But then reasonable isn't a word I often used in connection with Jock."

"I'll come by tonight," Grace said.

7

Peter Earp arrived at his Georgian-style home on Toronto's Bridle Path a little after six o'clock. Amy Wu-Chan was emerging from the walk-in shower as he entered the master bedroom. She said, "Washing her off."

"That bad?"

"I prefer you," she said, coming into his arms.

"But—"

"I don't have a lot of time." Amy kissed his mouth. "She's expecting me."

Amy turned to the bed one of Peter's lovers once had described as being the size of a helicopter landing pad. Peter started to undress. "What was that all about at the funeral home?"

"What was what all about?" Amy lay stretched out on the center of the bed.

"The Red Queen summoning Whitlock's niece."

"I'm not sure it was anything," Amy said.

"Come on. Eve Harriot doesn't brush her teeth without there being some sort of ulterior motive."

"You know, I'm supposed to be getting intel from you," Amy said.

"Are you?" Peter finished undressing.

"The mysterious Mr. Earp. Is he married? Separated? Does he have children? Does he like pizza with anchovies. Does he prefer Chinese or Thai?"

"I prefer you," he said, naked, padding over to the bed.

Amy smiled, admiring his trim body as he crawled across the bed to where she lay. "Well, well," she murmured. "Can he get hard simply by looking at a naked woman? Oh, look, he can."

He ran his hand down the length of her body.

Amy groaned and said, "Where did he come from? Why is he throwing his money around? Is he going to take over the world, or what?"

Peter kissed her breast. "If I was going to take over the world, I don't think I'd do it from Canada."

"You haven't told me if you're married," she said, fondling him.

"I was married."

"To that gangster Johnny Fish's daughter?"

"I was married to the daughter of Hamilton businessman John Pesce."

"Does he finance your company? Are those rumors true?"

He looked down at what she was doing. "You really are pumping me."

"Ha. Ha," she said. "Answer the question."

"I thought I was supposed to be mysterious," Peter said. "You seem to know all sorts of shit about me—or think you know."

"Does he?"

He trailed his mouth from Amy's breasts to the nape of her neck. "Is that what Eve thinks?"

"That's nice," Amy murmured. "Why she wants me to see you." Her breath had become raspy. "She doesn't want to be linked to organized crime in Hamilton, that's for sure."

"Tell her there are no links to organized crime in Hamilton."

"Do that some more, please."

"This?"

She nodded. "You fascinate her. The bad boy."

"You think I'm a bad boy?"

"A very bad boy."

"Not so bad," he said.

"And maybe you scare her a bit."

"Nothing scary about me. Just a guy trying to earn a living."

"I like the bad boy better," Amy said.

"Does Eve know about this?" Peter asked.

"I don't know that she doesn't know," Amy said. "It's not a subject for discussion."

"What happened in the car?"

She was making small sounds of pleasure. "That's so nice," she said. "Don't worry about the car. You have other obligations at the moment."

Peter laughed and pulled her on top of him.

Later, Amy raised herself up on an elbow and said, "Why are you so interested in that Whitlock woman?"

"Why are you so interested in my father-in-law?"

"Because he's a fucking gangster and my boss is the premier of the province."

"I'm curious, that's all. The controversial Mounted Police corporal who blows the whistle on the treatment of woman in the Force and for her efforts gets canned, comes back to Milton, causes a whole lot of trouble for her own uncle and gets him indicted for murder. What is it about her, anyway?"

Amy shook her head. "I have no idea why the premier wanted to see her. When I opened the door, she was giving Jean her card and saying something about needing to surround herself with more women like her."

"Didn't she make wild accusations about attempted rape and murder in Afghanistan."

"I think she was telling the truth," Amy said.

"Okay, but why would the Red Queen want anything to do with her? Seems to me Jean Whitlock is pretty toxic right now."

"So are you, Peter."

"Not at all," Peter said.

"Well, you damned well could be, couldn't you?"

"You underestimate me."

"I'm not so sure about that."

Amy rolled away from Peter saying, "All I know, she and Jock Whitlock were close at one time. There are all sorts of stories about what Jock was up to out there in Milton with your predecessor, Mr. Del Caulder. And there was the murder charge. Jean Whitlock was going to testify for the Crown so maybe she knows where Jock buried the bodies. Eve certainly would find that useful."

"Or dangerous," Peter added.

Amy got off the bed. "Could be that Jean knows something Eve thinks she should know. She's in the ass-protecting business, that's for sure, and she's very good at it."

With that, Amy disappeared into the bathroom, closing the door behind her. Peter lay on the bed, his breathing settling, contemplating what he had just heard. A couple of minutes later, Amy reappeared, dressed, everything perfectly in place as though nothing had happened. A marvel of engineering. Peter watched her admiringly from the bed. She gave him an impish look. "What?"

"You know what I can't figure out? I can't figure out whether I'm paying you or her."

"As long as you get what you want, what difference does it make?" Amy picked up her shoulder bag from where she had left it on the dresser.

"I still haven't got what I want," he said.

"You got me." Accompanied by another impish look.

"Not enough," he said. "I like you Amy but I'm under the gun to get this fairgrounds development under way. My investors are growing impatient."

"You mean your ex-wife's father in law. The gangster."

Peter sat up, his gaze not quite so admiring. "I keep telling you. John Pesce has nothing to do with my business."

"Personally, I don't give a shit," Amy said. "But you're going to have to be patient. Everything will be fine. Eve does what I want. She doesn't think she does but she does."

"Do me a favor. Find out what interests the Red Queen about Jean Whitlock."

"Why should I do that?"

"Because my darling, crafty fuck buddy, knowledge is, as they say, power. And down the road we might need all the power we can get."

"Look at that," Amy said coolly. "I was wrong."

"About what?"

She reached down to him. "A woman doesn't have to be naked."

8

Twelve Bankers Boxes, file folders neatly packed in each of them.

Jean with Grace's help quickly moved the boxes from her car into the living room. Once they were finished, Jean poured Grace a glass of wine and then Jean took her upstairs to the bedroom. "What do you think?" Jean asked.

"About what?"

"The carpet."

"I like it," Grace said.

"It's Moroccan. Cactus silk."

"Unusual."

"You don't think it clashes with the bathroom tile."

Grace studied the bathroom tile and then studied the carpet. "A bit," she said.

"Shit," Jean said.

They went downstairs and sipped the wine in the living room standing among the stacked Bankers Boxes.

"I imagine there are a lot of people who would like to know what's in these," Grace observed after sipping her wine.

Jean thought of the Red Queen. Aloud, she said, "I have trouble believing Jock was crazy enough to leave a paper trail."

"He was obsessive about keeping track of things," Grace pointed out.

"It's going to take a while but I'll go through the stuff and see what's there," Jean said. She heaved a sigh. "He's dead but Jock continues to crowd my life."

"He loved you." Grace spoke quietly, not looking at Jean. "Despite everything, he loved you very much."

"I doubt Jock loved anyone," Jean said. "Not even himself."

"You're wrong, Jean. You were the light of his life."

"Your ability to see Jock through those rose-colored glasses you constantly wear is quite amazing," Jean said.

Grace looked hurt, making Jean immediately regret what she had blurted out. "Sorry," she said. "I'd like to say it's the wine talking but I haven't had enough."

"It's all right," Grace said. "Jock hurt all of us. It's just that some of us are more forgiving than others."

"What are you going to do now?" Jean asked.

"I thought our acting mayor might want to keep me on for a while longer but apparently that's not the case."

"I'm so sorry, Grace," Jean said. "None of this is fair."

"I can understand, given my history with Jock. Besides, I'm not so sure I want to work with anyone else." Grace placed her hand gently on Jean's arm. "One final piece of advice before an old friend leaves."

"Sure," Jean said.

"Be careful," she said.

"You think I have to be?"

"Probably nothing but, as I said before, a lot of people might want to see what's in those boxes and they might be willing to stop their contents from becoming public."

Which made Jean suspect what she had always suspected about Grace: that she knew a whole lot more than she would ever let on.

————

After Grace left, Jean sat with her wine eyeing the boxes grouped around. The collected secrets of Jock Whitlock? The paper trail that marked the progression of a life misspent? She didn't want to know, the bile rising at the thought of going through this shit, having to deal with anything that she did uncover. She did not want any more of her family's dark past, the curse of Jock Whitlock threatening even in death. She wanted to get on with her life although she had to admit she didn't have much of a life to get on with. The Mounties wanted her back, at least they did before her uncle turned up dead creating a renewed firestorm of attention, her name always in the second or third paragraph of the news stories about the mayor's death. Whether they were so anxious to have her now remained to be seen.

Besides, Jean wasn't certain that was a life either. She had returned to her hometown thinking it a refuge. Instead, it had turned out to be the proverbial town without pity, a veritable house of unfolding horrors culminating with her uncle hanging from a lamppost.

Shit. Shit…*Shit*!

Okay, Jean thought. Enough of this. Time to quit feeling sorry for herself. Besides, she had to admit she was at least a little bit curious as to what might be contained in her uncle's boxes.

She leaned forward and flipped the lid off the nearest box to reveal the rows of file folders. The world before the computer hard drive. Or the cloud.

Randomly, Jean pulled out one of the folders and opened it on her lap. Piles of individually stapled gas bills dating back twenty years. Not exactly the stuff of scandal or likely to put anyone in jail.

She tried another box and another file. Telephone bills this time. Again, dating back twenty years. Lunch and dinner receipts in another file. A thick file containing the minutes of 2001 council meetings.

Tiring of the search almost before it had begun, Jean sat back, finishing her wine. There appeared to be a paper trail all right, one that carefully tracked the inherent boredom of being the mayor of an Ontario town. There might well be more headline-worthy revelations contained in these boxes, Jean mused, but not so far.

Thank goodness, she thought. Perhaps she might be spared more Jock after all.

The wine had made her a little light-headed. She must be getting old if a glass of chardonnay could do this to her. It was a rather big glass. She rose from the chair, stumbled and knocked against the stack of boxes. The top box fell to the floor, spilling its contents across the carpet.

"Shit," she said out loud. Now at least one box was in disarray. She picked up the box and that's when she saw the key taped to the bottom. It was attached to a medallion. Someone had used a Magic Marker to scrawl the number 239 on its surface.

She tore the key out of the box, holding it as she slumped back into the chair wondering, What the hell is this?

9

"And there is no suicide note, is that correct?" demanded Chief Walt Dunnell from behind his desk at Halton Police Headquarters where he ruled with what he liked to think was an iron fist. He was more or less alone in that thinking. "Then, what is it? Murder or suicide?"

"Doc Prescott has yet to say one way or the other," Mickey Dann said. He and Glen Petrusiak occupied chairs facing the chief's desk in what everyone in the department referred to as the Hot Seats. The chief's office was known as the Shithouse. If you were unlucky enough to be seated in these chairs in front of the chief, you knew you were in shit.

Mickey and Petrusiak were in shit in the Shithouse.

"He finished his autopsy a week ago," the chief said.

"He's considering a coroner's inquest," Petrusiak said.

"Jesus H. Christ," the chief responded. "Can't the old bastard make up his mind?"

"Doc's been doing this a long time," Mickey said. "He doesn't like to be pushed into anything."

"Jesus H. Christ," Chief Dunnell repeated. "I've got the goddamned CNN crawling up my behind, not to mention the local media, and Doc doesn't like to be pushed? The mayor of the goddamn town is found hanging from a goddamn lamppost and we don't know a week later if it's murder or suicide? Jesus H. Christ."

The chief's gaze riveted on his two detectives, his eyes small and black. Like smoldering coals, Mickey thought. He jabbed a finger in Mickey's general direction. "What's your take on this, Dann? Murder or suicide?"

"Makes life a lot simpler if it's suicide," Mickey stated, thus avoiding having to commit himself one way or the other.

"My vote is for murder," Petrusiak offered, apparently not wanting to be left out of the dead mayor speculation game.

Chief Dunnell didn't much like the unsolicited opinion. It caused him to scowl and drum his fingers distractedly against the edge of his desk. Finally, his face softened and he said, "Let's say it is murder, who have we got for possible suspects?"

"The town of Milton," Mickey said.

Petrusiak issued a snort of laughter. Chief Dunnell did not look amused. "Give me some names."

Mickey wasn't sure what to say. He had no names beyond a general sense that Jock Whitlock had lots of enemies. Whether any of those enemies would want him dead was another matter entirely. "Like I said, Chief, life's a lot easier if it's suicide."

"What about Jean Whitlock?" Petrusiak chimed in.

Mickey gave him a look but instead of scowling more, the chief's face lit with possibility. "What makes you think of her?"

"Yeah, Glen," Mickey interjected. "What the hell would make you think of Jean?"

Petrusiak ignored his partner and focused on the chief, pleased that he finally had his superior's attention. "Disgraced former Mountie, already implicated in the suspicious death of a fellow officer, the woman responsible for bringing murder charges against the uncle she hates. Could be a good fit."

Mickey was shaking his head as Petrusiak finished speaking. "You're saying Jean killed her uncle, then strung him from a light pole on Main Street to make it look like suicide?"

"I'm saying it's worth looking into if this turns out to be murder, that's all I'm saying." Petrusiak now sounded defensive.

Chief Dunnell aimed his gaze at Mickey. "Have you talked to Jean Whitlock?"

"Not about this," Mickey answered.

"Talk to her. If this is murder then either she's implicated or she might know someone who is."

Mickey groaned inwardly. What a great way to pursue a relationship with Jean: Hi, can I buy you a drink? And incidentally, did you happen to murder your uncle?

Shit in the Shithouse.

———

"Don't be pissed at me," Glen Petrusiak said to Mickey Dann as the two detectives walked back to their desks.

"I'm not pissed," Mickey said. Pissed.

"Even though she's your girlfriend—"

"She's *not* my girlfriend," Mickey interjected with more vehemence than he intended.

"Fine, whatever. I still think she needs to be talked to."

"I'll talk to her," Mickey said.

"I should be there, too," Petrusiak said.

"Let me handle it."

"Suit yourself," Petrusiak said with a shrug.

Mickey could tell his partner wasn't happy. But then Mickey told himself he didn't give a shit. Murder or suicide, however it played out, Mickey doubted Jean had anything to do with either.

But he would call her. Go through the motions. If nothing else, it was an excuse to reconnect. Whatever that meant. After the interrogation was over, he could ask her on a date. They could go to a movie or have dinner.

Yeah. Right. Fat chance of that.

At his desk he dialed her number. Jean answered after a couple of rings. Seated across the way, Petrusiak tried to look busy, pretending not to listen.

"Hey," Jean said.

"How are you?"

"Tell me, how am I? Any news?"

"Not yet, no."

"Doc Prescott hasn't issued a report?"

"They're talking about a coroner's inquest."

"You're kidding."

"That's what I hear. Nothing for sure."

"God, this is going to take forever." Jean sounded weary. Mickey couldn't blame her.

"I'd like to have a talk with you, Jean."

"That's nice. What? You're going to whisper sweet nothings in my ear?"

"Not this time," Mickey said.

Silence on the other end of the line. "I'm beginning to get the idea this isn't a personal call."

"Let's say I'd appreciate it if we could have a chat."

"What about?"

"Let's say further that it would be in connection with our investigation into Jock's death."

"You know I've already given a statement," Jean said.

"I know, but we're just trying to cover all the bases, you understand."

"Do I?"

Mickey dodged the question with a question. "How's tomorrow for you?"

"Tomorrow's fine," Jean said.

"Why don't you drop around here. Say, ten o'clock?"

"You want me to come to the police station?" Jean sounded surprised.

"A formality, that's all."

"A formality at the police station."

"I'll see you then, okay?"

The line went dead.

Petrusiak snorted out a laugh. "She hung up on you."

"She hung up, that's all."

"She hung up on you."

"Fuck you," Mickey said.

Seething.

———

To hell with him, Jean thought as she opened the refrigerator door and withdrew the chardonnay. Medicinal. Something to take the edge off talking to assholes. He doesn't call for weeks and when he does, it's to interrogate me.

Remember the first law of being a police woman: Whatever you do, do not get involved with a police man.

Even if you did date him in high school. Sort of date him. Well, he remembered a date; she couldn't quite remember.

To hell with him, she repeated to herself as she poured chardonnay into a wine glass.

The bastard. Mickey knew full well she didn't want to be dragged into this but here he was dragging her in.

She wasn't interested in him anyway, she told herself, repeating what she had told herself any number of times since returning to Milton. The last thing she needed right now was a relationship, certainly not a relationship with a cop. A cop who, by the way, thought she might be a suspect in her uncle's death. That was the only reason he would want to interrogate her at police headquarters. No way was this a formality. She was a suspect.

Bastard.

She carried her wine glass into the living room to once again confront the stack of Bankers Boxes. Should she tell Mickey about them? No, not for now. She had enough to deal with. She would tell him. But later.

Served the bastard right.

Her cell phone made the musical sounds announcing an incoming call. The readout said Earpland.

Earpland?

"Hello," she said into the receiver.

"Jean, it's Peter Earp. Do you remember me?"

"Yes."

"I'll get right to the point," Peter said, his voice businesslike. "I'd like to get together for a talk."

Another man who just wanted to talk, Jean thought ruefully. The world was suddenly full of them.

When Jean didn't immediately respond, Peter said, "Your availability this week."

"What about it?"

"How is it?"

"It's fine," Jean said.

"Toronto. My place. Thursday. 10 a.m. See you then."

Before she could object, to say she wasn't going all the way into Toronto for "a talk," he was gone. Startled at the speed with which she had been dismissed, Jean sat with the phone as though expecting him to call back. He didn't. Well, well, she thought. Sometimes you hang up on the jerk.

And sometimes the jerk hangs up on you.

10

The following day, Mickey Dann, in shirtsleeves, Glock 22 pistol attached to the belt of his jeans, ushered Jean into a tiny white-walled conference room at Halton Police Headquarters. He sat on one side of a table, his hands clasped in front of him, while Jean sat on the other. Or, more accurately, slumped in a chair in what she hoped was, simultaneously, a show of relaxation and hostility.

"Thanks for coming in today, Jean," Mickey said in his official police investigator voice. "If you don't object, this conversation is being recorded.

"That's fine," Jean said.

Mickey paused as though trying to think of what to say next. "First of all, for the record, please tell me your name and your relationship to Mayor Jock Whitlock."

Jean thought, Brother, this really is Mickey at his most officious, and then thought further that perhaps she should give him a break and realize he was merely following orders, playing it strictly by the book.

Okay. She could play it that way, too. "My name is Jean Whitlock. Jock Whitlock is my uncle."

"Jean, can you tell me where you were on the morning of May 15?"

"I was home in bed, probably asleep, although I'm not sleeping that well, lately," Jean answered.

"Is there anyone who can verify your whereabouts on that morning?" Mickey asked.

Jean forced herself not to snap back a smartass answer. Instead, in keeping with the formality of the occasion, she said, "No, I was alone."

"What can you tell us about the death of your uncle, Jock Whitlock?"

"I don't know any more than what I was told by police the morning I was informed of his death."

"Did you have any indication leading up to his death that Mr. Whitlock might be inclined to take his own life?"

"I have no idea," Jean said. "I had not spoken to my uncle since his arrest. I have no idea what his state of mind might have been."

"But from your knowledge of your uncle prior to his arrest, would you say he might be the type of individual who would take his own life?"

"I don't know what type you have to be to kill yourself," Jean said. "But as far as Jock was concerned, I would have to say he was not the type to do something like that."

"Then, in your mind, would it be more likely he was murdered?"

Jean couldn't hide her surprise. "I wouldn't say that at all," she said, choosing her words carefully. "That will be up to the medical examiner to decide."

The door swung open and Glen Petrusiak stepped in. "Mind if I join you?"

Without waiting for an answer, Petrusiak yanked a molded plastic chair into position and seated himself on it while Mickey's face darkened into a scowl.

"I've just got a couple of follow-up questions, if you don't mind," Petrusiak announced.

Mickey fell into a stony silence. Petrusiak ignored him and addressed Jean. "Good morning, Jean."

"Good morning, Detective Petrusiak." Interrogation room formal.

Petrusiak: "You stated earlier you were home in bed at the time of Jock Whitlock's death."

Aha, she thought, he was listening in another room. Another bastard. But then she already knew that about Petrusiak. Mickey was another matter. Sometimes he was a bastard, like today. But then sometimes he wasn't.

Out loud, Jean responded, "I'm not sure the medical examiner has even established a time of death. If he has, I'm not aware of it."

"Fair enough. Then can you provide any substantiation as to your whereabouts between say 11 p.m. that evening and 6:30 a.m. the following morning when the body was discovered?"

"Like I told Detective Mann, I was home. Alone."

"You didn't go out at all that night?"

"No."

"Then what you're saying, Jean, you're telling us you have no alibi for your whereabouts on the night and early morning your uncle was murdered."

"Is that what you're saying? That he was murdered?"

"Let's say it's a possibility," Petrusiak said.

"You want me to provide you with an alibi for a possibility," Jean said, keeping her voice level, remaining the professional in the face of Petrusiak's bullying. "I can't do that."

"I believe this is going to shortly become a murder investigation," Petrusiak stated. "If that turns out to be the case, Jean, then you should know you will be regarded as a suspect."

Jean stared at him. Mickey's scowl had deepened but he said nothing. Petrusiak in the meantime sat back in the chair unable to hide the satisfaction of his achievement. Exactly what that achievement was, Jean couldn't say

"Given your hostile attitude, Detective," Jean said, "I might as well give up in the face of your clever questioning and simply confess to stringing my uncle from a lamppost in downtown Milton. Just what anyone in my position would do if they wanted to knock off a relative."

"Is that what you're doing?" Petrusiak asked in a sober voice. "You're confessing?"

Jean gave him a look and then stood up. "You know, Detective Petrusiak, I've always had the sneaking suspicion you are an asshole. But until now, I never would have guessed you're a stupid asshole."

Petrusiak allowed a startled expression as she went out the door.

Jean, swallowing hard, trying to tamp down her anger, exited the police station and started across the parking lot. As she reached her car, a voice called out and she turned to see Mickey Dann. "Hold up a minute," he called a second time.

She paused, car keys in hand, as he reached her. "Sorry about what went on in there," he said, slightly out of breath.

"What the hell was that all about?" she demanded.

"I didn't have any choice, okay? That's what they wanted."

"What? You really think I'm a suspect?"

"Not me. But there are people in that building grasping at straws. They don't know what to think and there's a whole lot of pressure to get to the bottom of this. International media are breathing down everyone's neck. We're on CNN, for God's sake. Walt Dunnell is an idiot at the best of times. All this has thrown his idiocy into overdrive. As for Petrusiak, he sees an opportunity to do a little grandstanding, I suppose. I can tell you he wasn't supposed to be part of the interview."

"But he was."

"He's an asshole," Mickey said. "What can I tell you?"

"So are you," Jean shot back.

She got into the car, half expecting Mickey to say something in response. But he didn't. He just stood there.

Damn him, she thought as she drove away.

By the time she got home, Jean had cooled off somewhat.

She hated to admit it but maybe Mickey had a point. If she was still a police officer, she might have done the same thing, except she would have handled it better. The way Mickey and Petrusiak conducted the interview, it was a farce, Keystone Kops on parade. Those fools were never going to get to the bottom of what happened. That is, if there was a bottom to get to.

Jean got out of the car thinking she would have to do some grocery shopping, but later. Right now, she just wanted to take a deep breath and try to shake off the morning's unpleasantness at Halton Police Headquarters.

She unlocked the front door and stepped into the dim, cool interior. The fresh paint smell was still in the air.

But there was something else, too.

She closed the door behind her, and then stopped. She'd experienced this sense before, a feeling that the air around her had been disturbed by something that did not belong in the house.

She inhaled deeply, drawing in the faintest whiff of tobacco. It lingered around the edges of the fresh paint smell. Or was she imagining things? She took more breaths.

No, someone *had* been in here. She kicked herself for leaving her Glock locked away in her upstairs bedroom. A lot of help it was going to be up there.

She stopped breathing, standing still. Listening.

The silence roared back at her.

Slowly, she slipped off her shoes and, barefoot, started forward, placing one foot softly after another, moving into the living room. Nothing appeared to have been disturbed. Only one thing was noticeably different.

The Bankers Boxes.

They were gone.

11

At midnight, Jean sat in her living room with her second—or was it the third?—glass of chardonnay contemplating the empty space where the Bankers Boxes had been stacked. Who would have made off with twelve boxes of what basically amounted—or seemed to amount—to Jock Whitlock's old phone and restaurant bills as well as the minutes from long-forgotten town council meetings?

Whoever broke in and removed the boxes would not have known that. Unless, that is, the burglars knew something Jean didn't. Whatever it turned out to be, this was a problem Jean did not want in her life right now. The theft of those files meant that someone cared enough to go to a lot of trouble, indicating Jock was in possession of material someone did not want made public. Now it was up to Jean to either figure out who that someone was or turn this over to the police.

Turn it over to the Keystone Kops? Provide Glen Petrusiak with more incentive to believe she was somehow mixed up in her uncle's death when she wasn't mixed up at all?

Not until now, at least.

Something else troubled her: Someone *knew*. They *knew* about the files. They *knew* those boxes were in her house; they *knew* she was absent and so could get safely in and out.

That realization wasn't merely another problem. It was downright frightening. She was being watched.

Go to the police, right? No, not the police. It would be up to her to do something. She couldn't rely on anyone but herself. She never could, and that was fine. She had survived this long by trusting her own instincts and not much else.

Particularly where the male of the species was concerned.

Right now, her instincts were telling her to not say anything. Not until she had a chance to figure out who stole the files and why. About the last thing she wanted to do with her life. Her non-life, she amended, rising unsteadily and making her way to the kitchen with her empty wine glass.

Whoa, she thought, take it easy there, Jean. You're hitting the vino blanco a little harder than was healthy. She had to keep her wits about her. The wine glass went into the sink with a little more care than usual.

Jean made her way upstairs to her bedroom. She pulled the Treklite Lock Box, adjusted the tumblers to the four-digit combination and then opened it up. The Glock automatic lay inside.

She lifted out the Glock, checked the clip to make sure it was loaded and then placed it on the nightstand within easy reach beside her bed.

A girl can't be too careful, she thought.

———

When Jean opened her eyes the next morning, the first thing that came into focus was the Glock. Right, she thought as she sat up, a maneuver that caused the room to tilt at a German-expressionist-film angle. Maybe the wine last night caused her to overreact a bit.

But as she rose from the bed and started dressing in her jogging shorts and top, she had second thoughts—third thoughts? The rationalizations she had come up with the night before still applied in the cold light of day. She was being watched and if that was the case, she wasn't overreacting at all. Before leaving the bedroom, she installed the Glock under one of her pillows. Not quite so exposed that way.

She felt out of sorts as she reached the fairgrounds and began her morning run around the dirt track circling past the big stadium. The sky was overcast, the wind rising, rain threatening. The usual dog walkers were out, a variety of breeds running loose despite the town ordinance stating that mutts had to be leashed at a fairground deserted most of the year save for dogs and their owners.

And the occasional jogger such as Jean Whitlock, feeling better as she sucked in deep breaths rounding the curve of the track. She picked up speed as a black Porsche came into view through the main gate. Unusual to see a vehicle out here at this time of the day, she mused, let alone something as exotic as a Porsche.

She continued running, aware that the Porsche had turned onto the track and was coming behind her. Casting a glance over her shoulder, she saw that the Porsche had slowed, keeping a few yards distance, seemingly content to follow her. When she ran faster, the Porsche accelerated a bit, making sure to keep the same distance.

Irritated, Jean swerved off the track onto the grassy center median. Hands on her hips, she watched as the Porsche stopped on the track. The driver's-side door opened and Peter Earp squeezed inelegantly out, much to Jean's satisfaction. You could have the most expensive car in the world, but it didn't prevent you from looking like an asshole when you exited.

Peter wore faded jeans, cowboy boots, and an untucked white linen shirt; a rich hombre in his expensive car, coming through the dust as the morning sun struggled through the cloud cover.

"Can you believe it?" Peter announced. "All this prime land sitting empty in the middle of town."

Jean did not say anything.

Peter stopped a couple of feet from her. "What I'm going to do is transform this community. The Fairground. That's what I'm calling the development. High-end townhouses, beautifully designed. The downtown area is dying. The Fairground will bring it back to life. This is a multi-million-dollar project. My ass is on the line but that's okay. I'm going to make it happen."

"Good for you," Jean said.

"I'm not happy with you," Peter said.

"I don't really give a shit," Jean said.

"You were supposed to be at my office yesterday for a meeting."

"Was I?"

"We had an appointment."

"*You* had an appointment," Jean said. "I didn't."

"Christ, I've had to turn my whole schedule around to drive out here this morning." He indicated the Porsche. "Come on, get in."

"You've got to be kidding," Jean said. "I'm not going anywhere with you."

Momentarily, what she assumed was Peter's usual cockiness slipped. "Why not?"

"Because I'm going to finish my run."

"Well, Jesus Christ," Peter said with a touch of confusion. "Look, all right, finish your run and then at least let me buy you a cup of coffee?"

"The Ice Cream Lab in an hour."

"Where's that?"

"Main Street," she said.

"Okay, fine."

"And I'm not waiting around for you."

Jean turned away and resumed her run. This time, she noticed, the Porsche did not follow her.

12

Peter with a latte was seated in one of the booths when she arrived at the Ice Cream Lab an hour later, having finished her run, showered at home, and changed into street clothes. When she slid into the seat across from him, she noted the softening of his features, the almost physical attempt not to show impatience with her lateness. He asked her if she wanted anything. "The lattes here are very good," she said.

To her surprise, he got up and went to the counter and ordered the latte from the server.

"You're trying to be nice to me," she said as he re-seated himself.

"I schedule niceness at least twice a month," Peter said.

"Then I guess this is my lucky day," Jean said.

"We got off on the wrong foot," he said.

"We didn't get off on any foot."

Peter allowed the hint of a smile. The smile had the effect of removing some of the glowering sternness that he must have used to scare the peasants. "I'm trying to change that," he said.

"Why would you want to do that?"

The server arrived with Jean's latte and asked if they wanted anything else. Jean shook her head and then took a sip of the latte.

"How is it?" Peter inquired.

"It's fine," she said. "You haven't answered my question."

"Why would I want to be nice to you?"

"That was the question."

"Because I might be considering hiring you to do a job for me," Peter said.

"What would make you think I'm for hire?"

Peter shrugged. "Former RCMP corporal, lots of police experience. I understood you're available for private security consultations."

"Who would have told you that?"

He paused before he said, "Your uncle might have mentioned it during one of our conversations."

"Jock told you I was available for 'private security consultations?'"

"That surprises you?"

"It doesn't sound like Jock."

"Are you available or not?"

"You want to consult with me? Is that it?"

"Not quite."

"Then what?"

"A man named Max Flagg."

Peter waited to see if the name registered with Jean. It didn't.

"Mr. Flagg runs a Milton electrical company, at least that's what he says he does. In reality, he dabbles in a number of sidelines that include prostitution, illegal opioids, and—this is where I come into it—extortion."

"He's trying to extort you?"

Peter nodded. "He wants me to pay for something that if it's made public will ruin me in this town."

"Will it?"

"That's what I want you to find out," Peter said.

"What's your feeling?"

"My feeling is that this is a delicate time for me. I'm having to deal with the mayor, the town council. There's lots of opposition to what I want to do. Now I've got Max Flagg to deal with. The point is, I don't need any more trouble and Max sounds as though he could be trouble."

"You must have some idea of what he's got. Otherwise, why would you pay any attention to him?"

"Let's just say I don't want to take any chances."

"I'm not sure what any of this has to do with me," Jean said, suspecting she knew all too well what it had to do with her.

"I'd like you to find out what you can about this guy. Right now, I'm flying blind. It's hard to tell what kind of threat this guy represents. I'd like you to provide me with a risk assessment."

"If he's threatening you, you should go to the police."

"The police and the attendant publicity are the last things I need right now. Millions of dollars of development are on the line, not only at the fairgrounds but other projects as well that I inherited when I took over Del Caulder's company."

"And made it part of Earpland."

"I don't want any more complications."

"Well, we do share one thing in common," Jean said.

"What's that?"

"Neither one of us wants more complication in our lives. What you're describing is a big complication and I don't want that."

"Help me out, Jean. Keep it simple. Nose around a bit, that's all. See what you as an experienced professional can see." He seemed vulnerable as he added: "I'm not sure where else to turn."

"There are lots of investigative agencies around. Go to one of them."

"I can't count on their discretion. I think I can count on yours. Besides, you know this town. You know the people. You know your way around."

"Not as well as you might think," Jean said.

"Tell you what. Spend a couple of days on this for me. If you conclude this bastard is blowing smoke then I won't worry as much. If you get a sense there is more to it, then you'll have my thanks, not to mention a lot of money."

"I don't need your money."

"Everyone needs money," Peter said. He offered a ghostlike smile. "And I have a lot of it."

That was his cue to reach into his shoulder bag to extract a manila envelope. "Some background my people at the office have been able to put together about Max Flagg. Not much but it will get you started."

He slipped it across the table to her as though it was tempting bait. He placed a check on top of the file. "Ten thousand dollars should get you started."

"That's too much to just nose around," she said.

"Not if it gets results."

He put a Samsung smart phone on top of the check and the file. "Carry that with you the next while, if you don't mind. Hit the phone icon. That immediately connects you with me. An encrypted line."

"And how do you get in touch with me?"

He grinned and pointed at the phone. "I promise not to call too often."

"Supposing I say no?"

"I don't know you, Jean, but I'm willing to bet that no matter how much you try to deny it, the basic animal instincts of the hunt are built into your DNA. That's why, if your uncle was right, you defied everyone to become a police officer in the first place. I'm counting on you being intrigued enough, and missing the chase enough to do this."

"You're wrong about me," Jean said.

"Am I?"

She waited just long enough to perhaps scare him a bit. Then she picked up the check.

The ghostlike smile was back, a little more triumphant this time.

Bastard, she thought.

All men are bastards.

———

Main Street on a weekday afternoon was nearly deserted.

There were not many passersby to notice the parallel-parked white van and the guy waiting patiently in the passenger seat cradling a camera with a Nikon

400-millimeter zoom lens attached, the type used by bigtime photographers to capture the action at sporting events.

Sal had once entertained hopes of becoming a sports photographer but that aspiration had gone out the window at the age of twenty when he went to prison after trying to rob a bank. Everyone had told Sal that he was out of his mind to rob a bank in this day and age but to Sal there remained something romantic about bank robbery, *Butch Cassidy and the Sundance Kid* being one of his favorite movies. There was sort of a Robin Hood aspect to the whole deal, taking from the rich, who could goddamn well afford it, and giving to the poor—himself.

"Okay, here they come," Britney declared, tensing behind the wheel. An immense woman, Britney, barely contained in leggings and a leather jacket, her buzz cut recently dyed white. She gazed out the windshield, in time to see Peter Earp emerge from the coffee shop in the company of a woman.

Sal lifted his camera to get a shot of the two. The woman wasn't bad looking, Sal thought as he snapped off a photo. Not exactly the supermodel type Earp was usually seen with, but attractive for a woman who, from the look of her, didn't spend a lot of time worrying about her appearance. She didn't need to.

"Any idea who that is?" Britney asked as Sal continued snapping photos.

"No idea," Sal replied. In his view finder he could see that the woman carried some sort of file. What the hell was Earp up to? That's what they were supposed to find out but thus far they had come up with diddly squat.

On the street, the woman shook Earp's hand. Formal-like. Professional. Not the girlfriend type, Sal surmised. Some sort of business thing.

"Boss man will want to know who she is," Britney announced, unnecessarily in Sal's view.

"Boss man gets what he gets." Sal allowed himself to sound irritated, taking more photos as the woman got into her shit-box Ford. A woman who didn't look like a model, driving a crap car. Not Earp's style at all.

Sal was intrigued.

"Hey, what the hell you doing?" Britney demanding, shifting around her huge bulk in order to facilitate the delivery of one of her trademark dirty looks.

"What's it look like? I'm taking pictures, like I'm supposed to."

"You got your eye on that Miss Natural Bitch with Earp," Britney snapped. "You're pissing me off."

"I'm doing my job, Britney!" Sal yelled.

"Yeah, screw you, Sal. Your doing your job and I'm flying to the moon."

"Then fly to the moon for all I care."

Britney burst into tears.

13

A fire Jock probably set himself had destroyed the massive home he had been building on Derry Road. He and his wife Desiree had moved into a rented townhouse until their new place was rebuilt. Jean had no desire to go there but she was the executor of her uncle's estate, thus a visit was necessary if only to decide what to do with the contents.

And even though the police had already been through the place, Jean couldn't help but think there might be something in there that they missed, that a niece might stumble upon, that would help explain her uncle's death.

Explain the unexplainable, she thought as she sat in the drive. Unravel one more mystery in a life full of them. The file Peter Earp had provided lay in her lap. Two double-spaced pages. Not exactly a ton of material on Max Flagg.

Max's mug shot was clipped to the file, a heavyset, thug-like individual with a permanent five o'clock shadow, glowering into the camera, ready to screw the world given a chance. The perfect stock villain occupying a dark corner on the local landscape. As a police officer she would take one look at Max and know he had done jail time; that he was a habitual hardcore offender who knew no other life other than one that involved breaking the law.

Supposedly, Max Flagg operated Dynamic Electric, headquartered on Bronte Street in Milton, south of Steeles Avenue. The background material more or less restated what Peter had already told her, that the company was a front for a criminal enterprise run by Flagg that included everything from trafficking in illegal opioids to running an escort service in Burlington and Oakville.

And the extortion racket victimizing Peter Earp.

Max, somewhat to Jean's surprise since she had never heard of him, was a Milton native. He had been convicted of assault when he was nineteen; sexual assault a couple of years later, and a string of drug charges after that. He also had been arrested for attempted murder five years before but the charges had been dropped.

Even though he purported to own and operate an electrical company, there was no indication that he had ever worked as an electrician.

A real solid citizen, Max, Jean surmised ruefully, a credit to the community.

She closed the file and placed it in the glove compartment before getting out of the car, taking a deep breath, steeling herself to reenter the life of the late Jock Whitlock.

As soon as Jean stepped inside the vestibule, Jean saw that someone other than the police had been in here. Someone who had not carefully searched through the premises as the police would have, but who had ransacked the place.

Sofa cushions had been pulled off sofas. The anonymous country-scene wall paintings had been yanked out and thrown to the floor, their backs torn out. In the master bedroom, bedclothes were littered across the broadloom along with Jock's suits from the destroyed walk-in closet. The mattress had been yanked off the bed, the contents of dresser drawers spilled across the floor.

Jean took in the scale of the shambles in which the house had been left; the violence done to the evidence of a life lived, a person or persons unknown tearing through, looking for—what?

And who was doing the looking?

Her cell phone began to vibrate in her pocket. The readout said The Mayor's Office. Jock calling from a phone booth in hell?

With Jock, anything was possible.

"Jean Whitlock?" a female voice inquired.

"Yes, this is Jean."

"My name is Tamara Bal, Ms. Whitlock. I am the assistant to Acting Mayor Amar Bal."

"You have the same last name as the acting mayor," Jean noted.

"Yes, that is true. I am Mr. Bal's sister as well as his assistant."

Aha, Jean thought, the new Grace. Amar keeping it in the family. "What can I do for you, Ms. Bal?"

"The acting mayor would like to see you," Tamara said.

"I see. And when would the acting mayor like to do this?"

"This afternoon if possible."

"Yes, I suppose that's possible."

"Shall we say four o'clock at the acting mayor's office?"

"Sure. Four is fine," Jean said.

"I look forward to meeting you," Tamara said.

"I'll see you at four," Jean said.

What was that all about? Jean wondered as she put her phone away.

14

Tamara Bal, a beauty with a silky river of black hair flowing down her back, large, almost liquid eyes, didn't appear to be much more than twenty despite the austere business suit and white shirt buttoned to the throat, designed to provide the maturity she didn't possess. A far cry from Grace Travis, Jean thought as Tamara rose from her desk and said, "What a pleasure it is to meet you, Ms. Whitlock."

"Please, call me Jean."

Tamara graced the request with a smile and indicated the closed door to the mayor's office. "The acting mayor is waiting for you," as though this was a truly important event not open to everyone. With that, Tamara strode with brisk efficiency to the office door, threw it open, announcing, "Ms. Jean Whitlock, Mr. Acting Mayor, here to see you."

A quiet voice replied through the open door: "Send her in."

"You may enter," Tamara said, making a hand movement that indicated it was safe for Jean to move forward.

Amar Bal was already on his feet as Jean entered, coming around Jock's football field of a desk. Seeing him as he reached out his hand jarred her, so used was she to her uncle occupying this office.

Jock Whitlock always came to work in a bespoke suit and a tie in a perfect Windsor knot. Amar Bal wore a turban and a short-sleeved shirt tucked into khaki pants; the truly new man at the Town Hall, Jean thought as she took Amar's soft hand, nothing like her uncle's too-firm grip on everything.

"Thank you for coming," he said in a gentle, almost sonorous voice. Jock always said Amar's voice could heal the world. About as close as Jock ever got to wanting to heal the world, Jean thought. "Won't you take a seat."

Jean took the chair she had sat in a thousand times facing her usually stern-faced uncle. No sternness today; instead, Amar Bal's gentle face beamed from the thicket of his impressive beard. "You are probably wondering why I asked to see you."

"Actually, I've been meaning to get around for a visit, Mr. Mayor."

"Please." Amar made a dismissive gesture with his hand. "I stress to everyone I am the *acting* mayor. A humble *acting* mayor at that. I serve only until the next election, at which time the citizens of Milton will decide who it is they want to lead them."

"Then as acting mayor, how are you doing?"

Amar stopped to consider his answer, as though it was the first time he had been asked the question. And perhaps, considering the speed of recent events, it was. When he answered, Jean noted, his face beamed less. "I must be honest with you, Ms. Whitlock, I am not doing well."

Somewhat taken aback by his bald honesty in a place where, over the years, she had not heard a lot of honesty, bald or otherwise, Jean said, "I'm sorry to hear that."

"Everywhere I turn, I am faced with the evidence of your uncle's questionable actions while in office. I suspected some of this, I suppose most of us on the council did, but I had no idea of the immensity of his activities. I must say, I find myself in a continual state of shock, particularly in regards to his activities with the developer Del Caulder."

"Who is now in prison," Jean reminded him. "My uncle, had he lived, would have ended up in the cell next to him."

"For the murder of his wife, yes, I understand that."

"Had he been found guilty, that certainly would have been the most egregious of his crimes, unquestionably," Jean said.

Amar's coal black eyes bored into Jean, as though trying to see into her soul. Good luck with that, Jean thought. "Tell me, Ms. Whitlock, how do you feel about your uncle?"

"I don't feel good, obviously," Jean said. "I spent most of my life believing in things like honesty and the rule of law. I believed my uncle represented and believed in those values as well. I thought he was a good man. I was wrong on all counts."

"And so, Ms. Whitlock, may I ask how much can I depend on that sense of honesty and belief in the rule of law to help me root out the corruption in our town?"

The gentle voice so admired by Jock now contained an unexpected edge.

"I'm not sure what you mean," Jean said carefully.

"Mr. Peter Earp."

"What about him?" Jean asked, openly surprised.

"Mr. Peter Earp is no friend of this town."

"I don't know much about him," Jean said, more or less truthfully. "I know he bought out Del Caulder's company and therefore, added to what he already owns, he has become the Greater Toronto Area's biggest developer."

"His company Earpland spreads across this region like a disease, devouring good farmland for cheap, overpriced townhouse developments. Much of what he is doing was started by Del Caulder so there is little I can do to stop those projects. However, he now seeks approval for a townhouse development at the Milton fairgrounds. This I am determined to stop."

"So I've heard," Jean said.

"I would like to enlist you as part of my team to work together to stop this from happening." As he spoke, Amar's eyes lit with passionate fire. "This man is evil, perhaps worse than Mr. Del Caulder. Something evil has come this way, Jean, and it is in the form of Peter Earp."

"If you believe he's worse than Jock then that really is evil," Jean said.

"You think I am joking, Ms. Whitlock? I am not joking, believe me."

"I don't think you're joking," Jean said. "But I don't see how any of this involves me."

"This is how you can help me. He leaned forward; his hands spread out on the desk as though preparing to leap across it. "Use your skills as an experienced criminal investigator to get the information I need to stop this terrible man from digging his tentacles into the heart of our town. In pursuit of the fairground development, he is buying people, buying influence. But you know who he cannot buy, Ms. Whitlock? He cannot buy *me*." Amar's voice had risen to an angry crescendo.

"I understand what you're saying, Mr. Mayor, but I don't think you need my help to stop Peter Earp. The fairgrounds development idea has been around for years. It's this parcel of land, largely unused, sitting in the midst of downtown Milton, an easy target for developers. But even my uncle in cahoots with Del Caulder couldn't make it happen. If they couldn't succeed, I doubt Peter Earp can."

"Then I believe you underestimate the power of this man," Amar countered. "The idea you might have thought was dead is once again in play. Except I fear this time, unless we work to stop him, Peter Earp might well succeed. I beg you to help me, Jean."

"I don't know how I can do that," Jean said.

The frown that had been playing around the edges of Amar's face, deepened. "Why not, may I ask?"

"I'm not a police officer any longer. I have no investigative authority," Jean said. "Besides, this is not what I came back to Milton to do."

"I am asking you to help your community."

"I don't think my community needs me spying on people."

"You know people. You can discreetly ask questions that I cannot ask without attracting attention. Spend some time looking into his activities and report back to me. Maybe you find nothing but if you find something, I would like to know about it."

"My family is gone, I don't have a job, I'm trying to pull my life back together, and so far, not doing a good job of it. Spying for the mayor of Milton is the last thing I need."

As Amar considered this, his face regained its composure. He stroked at his beard and then said, "Here is what I know. I know you are a good friend of the community. I believe you do not want the corruption of the past. I further believe that if you hear anything, information I should know, you will get in touch." He smiled at her. "This is what I believe."

"Then let's leave it at that," Jean said. "If I hear anything that might help, I will be in touch."

Relief flooded Amar's face. He was beaming again, rising to come around to Jean. The hand of friendship was offered again. "Good of you to come, Jean," he said as she shook his hand. "I hope to see you again soon."

In the outer office, Tamara was on her feet, her smile as full of sunshine as her brother's. A couple of smilers, Jean thought. Jock would have cringed.

"Wonderful to finally meet you, Jean," she said. "I know you will help my brother in any way you can. It is most appreciated. I hope this is the beginning of many visits."

Jean had the uneasy feeling that the ghost of Jock Whitlock was following her out the door warning, "See? It wasn't just me. No matter who sits in that office, they're going to try and manipulate you to their own ends."

The ghost was certainly right about that.

15

By the time Eve Harriot arrived at the Forest Hill condo they shared together, Amy Wu-Chan had had their dinner waiting for over an hour: chicken breasts with fresh asparagus and a tossed salad, garnished with a side dish of smoldering unhappiness.

"Sorry," Eve said. "I couldn't get out of the meeting and then it turned out Pierre had a day off no one knew about so I had to wait around while they found a driver for me."

"You should learn to drive," Amy said pouring a glass of white wine and then handing it to Eve.

"I'm too busy serving the people," Eve said.

"You love being driven in a limo," Amy said. "You're from Thunder Bay. A limo means something to people up there."

"You're right. I do enjoy it. A tiny perk in a job that doesn't come with a whole lot of them."

"I'm a perk that cooks dinner for you and then sits around while it gets cold."

"You're the best perk of all," Eve said. She kissed Amy. "Thank you for being so understanding."

"I'm here to serve," Amy said.

"That's the spirit," Eve replied, and they both laughed.

Over dinner, as they usually did, they discussed the events of Eve's day, the mostly routine and mundane business of running a province: a visiting delegation from the Coalition of Indigenous Peoples not happy with her government; a tough question period, the opposition wanting to know why hydro bills were going up yet again; a press scrum during which the reporter from the *Toronto Star* all but accused her of lying to the people of Ontario, the prick. All in all, not a particularly good day but, hey, she got through, Amy said. The province was still here and they both had a job.

At least for the time being.

The wine and the nightly review, a good meal, usually helped Eve shake everything off and begin to relax. But not tonight, Amy thought. Even after a second glass of wine, Eve still seemed preoccupied.

"It's nothing," Eve insisted.

"I can read you," Amy replied. "There's something. What is it?"

"The *Star* asshole, maybe," Eve offered.

"No, that wouldn't do it. You have had too much experience with press assholes to let them get to you. Something else."

"Peter Earp," Eve said.

Amy fought hard to keep the look of surprise off her face, not succeeding. "What about him?"

"What he's doing out in Milton?"

"That's got you worried?"

"I don't know what he's doing; he's making noises like he's in trouble and if he is, that's potentially trouble for me."

"He's facing some challenges but we're going to help him and there's not going to be a problem."

"I could kick myself for what happened."

"It happened. Peter's cool with it. So am I."

"Maybe I wish you weren't so *cool* with it, as you say." Eve made a routine of folding her dinner napkin and straightening the silverware. A sure sign, Amy concluded, that things were nagging at her—personal things.

"Peter doesn't mean anything, you know that."

"Do I?"

Amy reached out her hand to Eve. "I like it better when there is no Red Queen, when it's just the two of us," she said. "No one else. Just us two. I'm selfish."

Eve clutched Amy's hand, a drowning woman reaching for a lifeline, Amy thought. "Me, too. We don't have enough of this."

"I love you," Amy said.

"I love you, too," Eve said. "Probably why I worry about Peter Earp."

"I keep telling you, Peter is not a problem."

Eve took her hand away. Her face darkened. "He knows a lot more than he should know."

Amy knew, too. That was her job; always stay one step ahead of the two of them.

That was the trick.

16

It was approaching ten o'clock by the time Jean got Jock's house back to a semblance of order: sofas and chairs straightened, cupboards closed, mattresses repositioned, discarded paintings if not rehung, at least leaned against the walls. All the time she worked, Jean wondered what it was that might have drawn intruders here in the first place. Either there was nothing or they took it with them.

For Jean, the house yielded nothing more than a reminder of the impersonal lives Jock and Desiree were leading while awaiting the rebuilding of the place on Derry Road. Or maybe it was the impersonal lives they led in general; the lack of personality, the absence of style or passion. Jock grasped for everything, Jean thought, but he left nothing.

Except a lot of turmoil.

An acting mayor—stress on the *acting*—who believed, thanks to Jock, evil had come to town in the person of Peter Earp. And maybe Amar Bal was right. Peter Earp apparently had drawn the attention of a low-life bad guy named Max Flagg, who could become an even worse nightmare for the acting mayor—a nightmare he wasn't even aware of.

And she was caught somewhere in the eye of the storm accompanied by a sense of guilt over the trouble created by her uncle and not happy at the thought of trying to do anything about it—experiencing feelings of regret that she had allowed herself to become involved with Peter Earp.

Yet, at the same time, intrigued.

Something was happening here and the police officer in her instinctively wanted to know what it was.

Against her better judgment.

The sound of the front door opening interrupted her reverie. She leapt to her feet, wishing she had brought the Glock with her. Footsteps sounded along the hall. A moment later, Grace Travis tentatively stuck her head around the corner. She looked relieved when she saw Jean. Probably as relieved as Jean felt.

"I'm sorry," Grace said in a weak voice. "I was driving by and saw the light on."

"Come on in, Grace. I'm just cleaning up."

Grace stepped further into the room. "What happened?"

"I think someone broke into the place," Jean said.

Grace's thin mouth formed an O of surprise. "Burglars, do you think?"

"Maybe, but I don't think so. Nothing of any value is missing. Someone was looking for something, I suspect. The question is, what were they looking for?"

"I can't imagine."

Jean thought that Grace could well imagine. That carefully arranged neutrality on her face that refused to show anything but which irritated Jean. "You know Grace, the thing I've always suspected about you and Jock…"

"There is no reason to suspect anything, Jean."

"I think there is plenty of reason to suspect you know a lot more than you are willing to admit to me or anyone else. Perhaps even to yourself."

"That's ridiculous," Grace said.

"You were his assistant and his lover, Grace."

"We weren't…" she could not quite get the word *lovers* out of her mouth. "I don't know what we were."

"You protected him for more than two decades. You know. Maybe you won't tell me but you *know.*"

Grace looked as though someone had slapped her face. "You—you've got the wrong idea about me and my relationship with Jock. I—I think I'd better go." She gulped out the words, on the verge of tears.

She started out, shoulders hunched, head down as though determined to plough through the storm and make her escape. Then, abruptly, she stopped. She turned to Jean, swallowed a couple of times. "There is one thing—and it's the *only* thing."

"What is it Grace?"

"I was going through some of his papers the other day and came across something I either wasn't aware of or hadn't really noticed."

"What was that?"

"A monthly charge on his private American Express account. Two hundred dollars for a storage space."

"That you didn't know about?"

Grace shook her head. "I don't know if it means anything."

"Was there an address?"

"No, but the name of the facility is A-Z Storage. I looked it up. It's on Martin Street. I even went around there to have a look."

"Did you go in?"

She again shook her head. "I didn't have a key."

Jean thought about the key she had found taped to the bottom of one of the Bankers Boxes. "Thanks for this, Grace."

"Let me say this for what's it worth," Grace said, her voice having strengthened considerably. "If you're expecting to uncover a big scandal in Jock's files, I believe you're going to be sorely disappointed. Jock was too smart to leave the kind of paper trail you or someone else might be looking for. If he wanted to hide something, it will stay hidden."

"I might believe you," Jean said. "But there are persons out there who don't, and they are after something."

"I have no idea what that could be." Grace's mouth tightened. Her face was transformed into a sullen mask. "I bid you good night, Jean."

She resumed her march against the storm.

———————

On her way home, Jean on impulse detoured onto Bronte Street North. A single light shone inside the fortress of concrete blocks that, according to the sign in front, housed Dynamic Electric. A low scrubby embankment ended at the chain-link fencing that enclosed the building. Jean could see a couple of vans parked at the side.

Jean stopped her car across the road. She could see that the light burned through the dust and grime of a front window. The place appeared locked up tight. If it was a front for a criminal enterprise, the criminals had gone home—or were out being criminals.

Well, maybe not all the criminals. As she watched, something stirred in the shadows behind the fence. Yellow eyes gleamed out of the darkness. A moment and then what looked like a wolf-dog faded into view. Its ears pricked back, the dog appeared to sense Jean as it came forward and then sat on its haunches close to the fence facing Jean.

Its jaws opened in a silent snarl.

A warning.

Her cell phone sounded on the seat beside her. When Jean swiped it open Peter Earp said, "I hope I didn't wake you."

"Just on my way home," Jean said.

"I thought I'd check in with you. Any news?"

Jean thought about it for a moment and then said, "I don't know if it's news but someone broke into Jock's house."

"How do you know this?" Peter asked.

"I was over there cleaning up the mess."

"Was anything stolen?"

"I don't know. Was there?"

That caused Peter to chuckle. "What? You think I broke into his house?"

"Not you. Someone working for you."

"You're working for me."

"Then you don't know anything about this."

"No." Peter sounded somewhat indignant. "It's absurd. Why would you even ask?"

"I guess I'm the suspicious type. People who had dealings with Jock might be worried about what he left behind. You might be one of those people."

"I try not to worry about anything. I try to control things. Then I don't have to worry."

"What about Amar Bal?"

Peter hesitated a tad too long, Jean thought, before he responded, "Milton's new mayor. What about him?"

"Acting mayor," Jean corrected.

"Am I supposed to be worried about him?"

"I don't know. I spoke to him today."

"I hope you told him I'm the best thing that ever happened to this town."

"I'm not sure he shares that view," Jean said.

"He's coming around. Why were you seeing him?"

"Tying up a few loose ends in connection with my uncle."

Again, there was too much hesitation. "No worries. Amar's a good man. I like him. We're working together on a number of projects."

"Are you?"

"He's being co-operative. A man who wants the best for Milton."

"Is that what you want, Peter? The best for Milton?"

"Like I said earlier, I'm great for this town. There are certain people who don't see that at the moment but they'll come around when they see the benefits of a development like The Fairground. Right now, though, I need to know about Max Flagg."

"I can tell you at midnight he keeps a big snarling dog at his place behind a chain-link fence."

"Where are you?"

"I'll be in touch," Jean said.

And hung up.

Interesting, Jean thought as she started along Bronte Street. Amar Bal thought Peter Earp was evil incarnate, an evil spawned by Jock Whitlock. Peter Earp, on the other hand, maintained that Amar was a friend who would only too gladly help him develop Milton.

Somewhere in between those two statements truth could be found, Jean thought.

But where?

17

The next morning, Jean was still in her pajamas, finishing her second cup of coffee, when there was a knock on the door. She was surprised to see Mickey Dann in the doorway. "Have you come to arrest me?" she asked, ushering him inside.

"Not today," Mickey said. "Is that coffee I smell brewing?"

"Would you like a cup?"

"If you're pouring."

He followed Jean into the kitchen. She said, "If you're not going to arrest me then what is it?"

"Maybe I just need a cup of coffee," Mickey said.

"Starbucks is closer."

"As it happens, I'm a Tim Horton's kind of guy."

"I might have known." She set a mug in front of him. "You take it black as I recall."

"And you have no sugar if I remember correctly."

"You do remember correctly."

She settled into a chair with her coffee, looking at him, raising her eyebrows in expectation.

"I thought you should know," Mickey said.

"Know what?"

"Doc Prescott has decided to convene a coroner's jury to investigate Jock's death."

"I guess I shouldn't be surprised," Jean said.

"The guy's chicken shit. He's reluctant to call the death of a controversial public official a homicide so he brooms it off to a jury to make the decision for him."

"He has the legal basis to do this, I assume."

"It's shaky. He claims that even though he was out on bail, Jock technically was still in custody at the time of his death, grounds for an inquest."

"What does Doc's decision mean for you?"

"The chief wants us to continue to gather evidence but without a clear sense of whether a crime has been committed, it's difficult."

"Any leads so far?"

"Nothing I feel comfortable talking about." Mickey sipped at the coffee and made a face.

"Don't like it?"

Mickey managed a smile. "If you don't mind my saying, you make a lousy cup of coffee."

"Don't ask me to cook dinner for you, either."

"I'll keep that in mind," Mickey said.

She gave him what Mickey might have described as a dirty look and then asked, "What do you know about a guy named Max Flagg?"

That caused Mickey to look up sharply from his coffee. "Why do you want to know about him?"

"Any reason I shouldn't?"

"Is this in connection with your uncle?"

"It's a name I've heard around," Jean said. "Obviously you know him—or know of him."

"The Electrician, that's what they call him. I know him all right. Charged him with murder five years ago when I was with Toronto homicide. He managed to slip the noose that time."

"He's out here now," Jean said.

"Always was. He happened to whack some poor son of a bitch in Toronto, that's all. A *real* bad actor. I mean a real bad actor. I'd love to know what he has to do with your uncle."

"I doubt he had anything to do with Jock."

Mickey eyed her suspiciously. "I don't like it when you lie to me."

"There's no reason to lie to you, Mickey. Curiosity, that's all."

"Whatever you're up to, be careful. This guy is no one to fool around with."

"I'm not up to anything," Jean said, not sure if she was telling the truth.

Mickey delivered a final frown at his coffee cup and then stood up. "I'd better be going."

"That's it? You show up at the door, insult my coffee, warn me not to get involved with local gangsters, and then leave?"

"You know, our last encounter…" His voice trailed off. "I wanted to make sure there are no hard feelings."

"No hard feelings. Interesting choice of words."

"And that you're still talking to me."

"Barely," Jean said.

"But talking. That's a good thing. Right?"

They stood, awkwardly facing one other. For a crazy moment, Jean thought he might kiss her. But the moment passed. He resumed the professional demeanor he would have used if he had been there to arrest her.

"Listen, if you hear anything or find anything in connection with Jock's death, you'll let me know. Right?"

"Sure," Jean said.

"That doesn't sound convincing."

"I doubt there's anything to share but if there is, I'll let you know."

They hesitated some more, neither certain what to say. "I'll keep in touch," was all Mickey could finally come up with.

"Great," Jean replied.

After Mickey left, Jean felt curiously disappointed. Disappointed in what? she asked herself as she poured more coffee. What did she expect from Mickey, anyway? Or more to the point, what did she *want* from him.

No idea, really.

She probably should have been—what?—more positive? Yes, that was it. Less the smartass who didn't care. Except, she *was* a smartass. It was up in the air whether she cared one way or the other. She was far from certain if she wanted to be attracted to anyone at this stage, even if it was Mickey Dann.

Who she was attracted to. Wasn't she?

The unanswered question. Perhaps unanswerable.

"It remains what it has from the beginning, a suspicious death," Doc Prescott said when Jean got hold of him. "The autopsy doesn't show anything other than Jock was strangled. Did he do it himself or did someone do it to him? I can't tell. Better to let a coroner's jury look at the evidence and decide for themselves."

"But if he killed himself, how did he get up on the lamppost?" Jean asked.

"Good question. I don't know. That's not for me to decide," Prescott said. "That's for the police."

"Who are waiting for you."

"There you go. The rock and the hard place. Thus, the coroner's jury, and we can all cover our asses."

"Meanwhile, if there is a killer, he's still out there."

"Nothing to stop the police investigation from continuing." He paused before he went on to say, "Or you, for that matter."

"I'm not in the murder business any longer," Jean said.

Doc Prescott chuckled. "Yeah, right. I don't know for certain, but my guess is that you're out there snooping around. And that's good. Except maybe for Mickey Dann, I don't trust these local cops. You can do a much better job."

"I'm not so sure about that," Jean said.

"Goodbye, Jean." Doc Prescott laughed one more time before he hung up.

Except, Jean reflected, how do you investigate a murder when no one's certain there *was* a murder? Even if it is the mayor, that was probably what the police were thinking. Why do anything when questions lingered as to what to do if you did something?

She would, she decided, do something. Anything was better than sitting around doing nothing. She climbed the stairs to her bedroom. The Glock was beneath one of the pillows on her bed. She checked the clip and then tucked it into the small of her back. She put on a leather jacket, and retrieved her police baton from the closet along with a balaclava.

Downstairs, Jean grabbed a bottle of water and went out to the car. She got behind the wheel and started the engine.

Movement creating action, she thought as she drove onto the street. She was already feeling better.

18

In bright daylight, Dynamic Electric looked anything but.

It sat sadly behind its chain link fence on a weedy wedge of embankment below railroad tracks. Someday soon, a developer would arrive to end its misery and replace it with a gleaming condominium complex. But, for now, this concrete pillbox survived and added to the neighborhood blight.

The entrance gate was open. There was no sign of a yellow-eyed wolf dog as Jean got out of her car and approached the building.

The yellow-eyed wolves were probably inside.

Well, not quite. As Jean came through the entrance, a bleached blonde woman with a lined smoker's face removed the cigarette from lips glistening with red lipstick, coughed without covering her mouth and asked, "What can I do for you, honey?"

"I'm looking for Max," Jean said.

The woman arranged her face to reflect her apparent puzzlement. "Max?"

"Max Flagg."

"No one by that name here, honey. What? You looking for some electrical work?"

Jean nodded. "A friend told me to mention Max's name if I needed a job done."

"What sort of job would that be?"

"The kind of job my friend said Max could handle, no problem."

"This friend of yours, does he or she have a name?"

"Jock Whitlock."

The woman appeared to consider this and then shrugged. "I'm confused, honey. You need electrical work done, you've come to the right place. Otherwise, I don't think I can help you."

"You don't?"

"You a cop by any chance?"

"Nope," Jean said.

"You look like a cop," the woman said.

"You don't like cops?"

"Oh, sure," the woman said dryly. "Everyone around here likes cops."

From the back, a big dog padded into view. Jean thought it must be the dog from the other night, only in daylight he didn't have yellow eyes or look much like a wolf.

"Hey, there fella," Jean said to him. "How are you doing?"

The German Shepherd cocked his head and looked inquiringly at Jean.

The woman behind the counter frowned. "Otis, get the hell lost."

The dog immediately lost the welcoming expression Jean was certain she could see on his face. Instead, he looked downcast as he slunk away. Jean felt sorry for him.

"Goddamn, dog," the woman mumbled.

"What's wrong with the dog?"

"He's a shitty guard dog, that's what's wrong with him. The only German Shepherd in the world who thinks he's everybody's friend."

"He does look friendly," Jean said.

"He should be tearing your throat out," the woman said.

"I tell you what," Jean said. "I'll leave you my cell phone number."

"Don't think it's gonna do much good."

"I'll leave my number," Jean said.

"Suit yourself, honey." A notepad appeared in the woman's hand. She dropped it on the counter in front of Jean.

Jean picked up a pen and scrawled her phone number on the notepad. "Tell Max that Jean dropped around and would appreciate it if he could get in touch as soon as he can." Jean pushed the note pad toward the woman.

"Did I mention there's no one here by that name."

"You did," Jean said.

"You still look like a cop to me."

Jean walked back into the yard as a banged-up white van with Dynamic Electric painted on the side pulled to a stop. Two rough-looking hombres got out. They had beards, hair down to their shoulders, wearing jeans and leather jackets. One of the men leered at Jean and said, "Hey there, aren't you something else." The other guy laughed and shook his head as they passed and went inside.

Assholes, Jean thought. *Men*, she thought further.

Down the street from Dynamic Electric, Sal moved his camera into position as he watched Jean exit the building and pass a couple of sketchy looking dudes, the kind of morons he had to put up with in prison. If that wasn't some sort of crime hangout, Sal decided, then he would eat his goddamn hat. Whatever eating your goddamn hat meant. Since he didn't have a goddamn hat.

When he stated his conclusion to Britney, behind the wheel while he rode shotgun and took the photos, she shrugged and said, "You know more about this shit than I do, jailbird."

"The question is, what's our new pal doing there," Sal said. He raised his camera with its awesome telephoto lens and snapped a couple of pictures as Jean got in her car.

"And how does she fit into Peter Earp?" chimed in Britney.

"That's what we're trying to figure out."

"When we should be out here focusing on Earp," Britney amended.

When Sal failed to respond, Britney added: "You've got the hots for this chick."

"Bullshit," said Sal.

"What is it with you, anyway? For all we know she needs some electrical work done. Big deal."

"Nah," Sal said with certainty. "You go to a shithole like that for a lot of different reasons, the least of them being you need an electrician. If there's one electrician in there I'll—"

"I know, I know," Britney said with a resigned sigh, "you'll eat your hat."

19

As Peter came along the hospital's bright hall, there was a stirring near the far end at the entrance to Kayla's room.

John's security people appeared, three of them, glaring as he approached. He came to a stop, not because he was afraid but because he did not want to create a scene and possibly upset Kayla, although these days nothing much would upset her.

A moment later, Monica swept into view, tall and lithe, her face drawn. When she saw Peter, her eyes went cold, her full mouth clamping shut, instantly transformed into a straight line of resistance as she flew past Peter without a glance in his direction.

A man taller than Monica emerged from Kayla's room. In his tailored Armani suit setting off the perfect Hermes tie, the elegance of John Pesce was on full display, an elegance he carefully nurtured possibly to offset the nickname his Hamilton friends had bestowed on him: Johnny Fish.

His daughter did not want anything to do with Peter except to hang onto his surname in order to spare herself the necessity of going back to her maiden name, Pesce, and all the perceived embarrassment that involved.

Well, he was happy that he could still be of some use to Monica. Even if she did hate his guts.

John Pesce, unlike his daughter, was unaccompanied by bodyguards and, also unlike his daughter, he stopped when he saw Peter. But similar to his daughter, Johnny Fish's eyes were hard, if not harder than his daughter's as they took in Peter. He carried a Gucci bag. John Pesce, Johnny Fish, was a Gucci kind of guy.

He motioned for Peter to come forward. Peter followed him to an alcove at the end of the hall.

"How's Kayla doing?" Peter asked. He knew full well how she was doing but at least it broke the ice a bit. John made a resigned gesture with his hand. "You know, what can I say? It is what it is. A tragedy. A goddamn tragedy."

He looked at the bag in his hand seeming to realize for the first time that he was carrying it. He thrust it at Peter as though it was too hot for him. And perhaps it was.

"Thanks, John, this is much appreciated," Peter said, taking the bag.

"You're getting yourself in pretty deep, Peter," John said.

"It'll be fine. Things are starting to come together in Milton."

"Are they?"

"This will certainly help," Peter said. He lifted the bag as if presenting the evidence of his claim.

"I hear there are problems. The mayor strung up on a lamppost. All that shit."

"It doesn't change anything."

"I thought he was your guy there."

"There are other guys," Peter assured.

"When I think about it, I don't know why I'm doing this," John said. "My daughter hates you, my granddaughter is lying in there close to death. I despise you with every bone in my goddamn body, yet I keep saving your sorry ass. I don't get it."

Peter remained still, hardly breathing, fearing that anything he said would only add gasoline to the fire.

John shook his head and then jabbed a finger at him. "But this is it, Peter, the end of the gravy train. You make this work, understand? I don't want to get into a lot of bullshit threats. I'm trying to run things as a business, although every time I turn around it seems I have to run it the way I used to run it, and that's no good. You're probably just as much a crook as I am so you're hardly the poster boy for legitimacy."

"The Milton development is legit, John. The Fairground is good for both of us. A great investment."

"Then let's see it pay off. The time has come for results."

"Yes, I understand," Peter said.

"Make sure you do," John said. He stepped past Peter saying, "Go in there and spend some time with your daughter. She needs you. God knows how much time she has left."

John Pesce went off along the hall, shoulders hunched, a big, sad man departing.

A dangerous man, Peter thought, forget all that shit about legitimacy, they were no more than words. Johnny Fish was an old-time Hamilton bad guy through and through, more than capable of killing anyone who crossed him.

Even his former son-in-law.

Peter entered the ward's darkened interior. Hooked up to all sorts of wires and tubes to keep her alive, Kayla was all but lost in the hospital bed where she lay. Her eyes flickered a bit as he bent to kiss her damp forehead. He pushed back a loose strand of her hair. Her eyes fluttered again. He told Kayla how much he loved her. He said he loved her more than anything in the world.

Then for the next hour, he sat holding her hand, the Gucci bag on the floor beside him.

———

Peter placed the Gucci bag on the ground beside him as he sat on a bench in High Park, taking in the afternoon sun.

Platoons of young mothers pushing elaborate strollers containing perfect children flowed past. Dog walkers struggling with an array of sniffing, barking mutts; oblivious teenagers on skate boards; solemn joggers; bike riders who, no matter how hard they tried not to, still managed to look goofy in their multi-colored nutcase helmets.

The passing afternoon parade. Peter enjoyed this, the chance to just breathe, feeling the warmth of the sun, thinking of his daughter, choking back more tears, focusing instead on the satisfying sense of not being bothered for a few minutes, at least not until he spotted her.

She wore a tan trench coat—perfect for the subterfuge in which she was a participant—hair pulled back, looking nervous. She was never going to cut it as a secret agent, Peter thought.

He called to her: "Tamara, over here."

Tamara Bal jumped as though struck by lightning, spotting Peter, relief flooding that clear, lovely face. She hurried over to where Peter sat.

"You scared the shit out of me," she said sitting beside him.

"I was beginning to wonder if you would show up," Peter said.

"The traffic coming into town was awful—as usual." She gave him a look. "And you're only going to make it worse."

"What? The world? Or just the traffic?"

"Probably both," she said.

"As I keep telling anyone who will listen, people need a place to live. That is the bottom line of our existence, the necessity of our lives, and that is what I provide. Nothing more harmful than that."

"Yes, well, try to tell that to my brother," Tamara said.

"I've tried," Peter said. "Now it's up to you."

She made a face. "I'm really feeling uncomfortable if you want to know the truth."

"Listen, you need help and thankfully, I'm able to provide it. Like I told you, no strings attached."

"If my brother knew about this, he would kill me."

"Amar won't know."

"I mean, he pays no attention to finances," Tamara said. "He's just so oblivious to everything except his work. He doesn't know how much trouble we're in."

"Obviously, he doesn't know about your gambling debts."

"Bastard." She slapped him lightly on the arm. "Nobody knows. I shouldn't have told you."

"But you did. Just be glad I'm in a position to help you."

Peter reached for the Gucci handbag, lifted it up and then put it down between them on the bench. "There. Now you're not in trouble. Simple as that."

She gave him another look. "I'm not naïve, Peter. Nothing involving money is as simple as *that*."

"The money is clean, but I don't want to take any chances. Your favorite casino isn't fussy about this sort of thing. At the cashier's cage, use your cash to buy chips. Spend a couple of hours, play some blackjack. Your favorite from what you tell me, and, hey, you might even win. Take your chips back to the cashier, trade them in for a check made out to cash, and then simply deposit it into your account. That way, there won't be questions about the mayor's sister depositing a suitcase filled with money."

"You've told me all this before."

"Just making sure, that's all."

He reached across and kissed the base of her neck. "Don't," she said.

He kissed her mouth.

"God," she said. "Kissing men in public, receiving bags of cash—"

He kissed her again. She looked around. No one was paying them any attention. Everyone was preoccupied with their own lives.

This time she kissed him.

Across the way, Sal, in a pair of cargo shorts and a floppy hat, aimed his camera with its telephoto lens in the direction of the two lovers on the park bench. When the woman kissed Peter a second time, Sal grinned with satisfaction and fired off a series of shots.

Sometimes this job did have its moments, he thought.

20

Promptly at six, the two sketchy hombres Jean had seen earlier emerged from the cinderblock building that housed Dynamic Electric, got into a shit-box truck and drove out of the yard, down the street, passing Jean.

Twenty minutes or so later, the woman behind the counter came out and got into a Toyota Prius and drove away in the opposite direction. Jean was just thinking that there was no one left inside when a heavyset man appeared. He spent a couple of minutes locking the front door and then went to a gleaming black Dodge truck and got inside.

This, she decided, must be Max Flagg.

And then she decided further that she would follow him. Not because that's what Peter Earp wanted her to do but because that's what she had become in her life.

A follower of bad people.

This particular bad person was blessed with a lengthy criminal record, easy for Jean to rationalize tailing him as he drove north on Highway 25. In the dimming evening light, storm clouds gathering strength overhead, Jean kept the truck's taillights in view.

Max turned onto a paved county sideroad but soon took a right onto a gravel road that curved up a hillside, past empty fields awaiting either the farmer's plough or, more likely these days, the developer's earth movers.

It began to rain as Max slowed for a turn onto a dirt track meandering to a two-story farm house perched on a hilltop. A tumbledown barn, partially ringed by collapsing deer fencing was visible behind the house. Jean parked at the side of the road. She could make out Max's truck, but there was no sign of the bad guy himself.

From the darkened farmhouse came a single, high-pitched woman's scream. And then silence.

Jean listened intently, debating what to do. Was she imagining it? Then a short, sharp shriek of pain. She hurried back to the car, retrieved her gun and the police baton from the glove compartment along with—a last minute decision—the balaclava.

Swinging left so that she came toward the house at an angle, Jean made her way up the hill, reaching a graveled yard with a tool shed at its edge, not far from a rusted tractor no one had driven for a long time. A light shone in the farm house's side window.

Presently, Jean heard more cries. A keening, begging voice. Jean raced around to the front of the house, pulling on the balaclava as she reached the entrance.

The door was open. She pushed into a dimly-lit hallway, nostrils filling with a rancid odor. To the left, a living room full of worn furniture, piles of clothing everywhere.

And a baby.

The baby was in a car seat on a sofa surrounded by heaps of laundry. The baby focused wide, saucer eyes on Jean as she stopped to look at him. A scream from the other room followed by the sound of hysterical weeping.

Jean snapped open her police baton, moving into the kitchen, also a mess. Jean was vaguely aware of a sink full of dirty dishes. An ironing board, an iron perched on its edge. Nearby, a young woman, naked except for a pair of panties cowered beside the stove. Blood streamed from her nose and mouth. Max Flagg's back was to Jean, his huge body tense, fist raised. The woman on the floor cried again. Jean called out, "That's enough."

Max's body tensed. He swung around, the surprise showing on his face an instant before it descended into black rage. The rage evaporated when Jean's baton lashed across his face.

Max was just like any other cheap hood, Jean thought, he bled and cried and didn't look nearly so tough as he went spinning back, crashing against the ironing board, sending the iron flying.

Vulnerable, Jean thought as she hit him again. He screamed and Jean used the end of the baton to poke him hard in the solar plexus. Max went down on the floor, gasping for breath. Jean stepped past him and grabbed the young woman's arm, lifting her to her feet. The woman wobbled, Jean held her, steadied her, saying, "Go to your baby. Get outside."

The woman looked dazed not knowing what to do. Jean pushed her forward. "Go," she ordered.

Max was struggling to his knees. Jean struck him again. He shook his head violently then regained his feet, his bulk filling the kitchen. He curled a fist the size of an anvil. He swung at her; she ducked but the fist managed to catch the side of her head. Jean fell back, seeing stars, trying to maintain her balance, failing, tumbling back onto the linoleum floor. Max loomed over her, shouting something she didn't catch. Her foot shot into his groin. He howled again, crashing against the wall, allowing Jean to sit up, desperately trying to clear her head.

No time.

Max in a rage was on the attack again. Jean's hand touched something on the floor. An iron. She kicked out at Max but this time he managed to dodge her foot. However, Jean had time to rise up, swinging the iron into Max's face. His nose exploded in blood. He sank to his knees holding his face. Jean swung the iron down on him hard, knocking him sideways to the floor.

The great Max Flagg, finally at rest.

Jean wondered if she might have killed him as she picked up the baton and staggered out of the kitchen along the hall. There was no sign of the woman or the baby, but the front door was open.

Jean found the woman reeling in the yard, whimpering incoherently, holding the baby seat with the child in it. Jean came to her, wrapping an arm around her, saying, "It's all right. It's going to be fine. What's your name?"

The woman stared with wild, fearful eyes and Jean realized she still wore the balaclava. She pulled it off and repeated, "Your name?"

"Blair Lalonde," she managed to say. "Who are you?"

"Someone who's going to make you and your baby safe," Jean said. "My car's down the road. Can you make it?"

Blair nodded. Jean removed her jacket and draped it around Blair's shoulders. Then she gently took the baby seat from her. Blair again looked frightened. "It's all right," Jean said. "Tell me the baby's name."

"Andy."

"Andy's going to be fine. We all are. But right now, we have to leave. Are you okay with that?"

"He's going to kill us both," Blair said in a weak voice.

"No, he's not," Jean said.

Together, with Jean holding the baby, they went down the darkened road. Jean used the flashlight on her cell phone to guide the way. By the time they reached the car, the baby had begun to cry. Jean opened the rear door and placed the seat in the back. That seemed to settle the child somewhat.

Jean helped Blair into the front, then went around and got in the driver's side and started the engine.

To her relief, Max Flagg failed to do what she feared he would do: come charging out of the darkness down the roadway. Just as well, Jean thought.

If he had, she would have shot the bastard.

21

Jean pulled into the Wal-Mart off Steeles Avenue.

Blair remained in the car while Jean ducked inside and quickly bought everything baby she could think of: diapers certainly, formula, clothes for a three-month old, piling a shopping cart full of things, desperately trying to wrap her head around a subject with which she had never before had to deal: a baby's needs.

On the way to checkout, she added a pair of women's jeans, a half-dozen tops, underwear that she hoped would fit Blair.

When they got to her house, Jean retrieved her first aid kit from the upstairs bathroom and then went to work cleaning the blood from Blair's face and nose, applying antibiotic ointment, taking particular care with the nasty gash on her forearm before applying a gauze pad and then bandaging it with adhesive tape.

Blair struggled into the jeans and one of the tops, going through the motions, silent, except when Jean asked her something pertaining to Andy. Blair answered in disinterested monosyllables.

Dressed, and looking a little more relaxed inside the safety of Jean's house, Blair fed her baby and changed his diaper. Then she got him into the red Sleepytime pajamas Jean had particularly liked but about which Blair appeared ambivalent. Blair appeared ambivalent about everything. She was here, Jean thought, but not really here at all; somewhere far away, in a world of her own.

Once the baby had been wrapped in a blanket and set down on the sofa where Jean and Blair could keep an eye on him, Blair turned curious eyes on Jean. "Why did you do it?"

"Do what?"

"This. Helping me."

"He was beating the shit out of you, Blair. You have a baby. Why wouldn't I help you?"

Blair shrugged. "Okay."

No thanks or anything. Just, "okay."

Jean asked, "What was Max doing there?"

"Like you said. Beating the shit out of me."

"Why would he do that?"

"He was looking for Jimmy."

"And Jimmy is?"

"My shitass, no-good boyfriend."

"That's Jimmy who?"

"Jimmy Boyd. Only now he's disappeared and I don't know what's happened to him. I was there waiting for no-show, unreliable asshole Jimmy when Max drives up. I think he's got news about Jimmy. Instead, he flies into a rage accusing me of talking to the cops, which isn't true. Then he's hitting me and you turn up in that mask like Zorro or whatever and start beating up Max, who is even more of an asshole than Jimmy."

She gazed at Jean with what looked a bit like admiration. "I mean, I never saw nothing like that before. Like, where did you come from and what were you doing there?"

"I'm doing some investigative work that involved following Max," Jean explained.

"What are you? A cop?" The fear was back in Blair's eyes.

"I used to be. Not anymore," Jean said. "Not for a while now."

"Well, I appreciate what you did for me and everything but now Max is going to be doubly pissed thinking that I'm talking to the cops."

"What would you be talking to the police about, Blair?"

She shrugged and looked away. "I dunno. Drugs, I guess. What else do you talk to the cops about when it's a guy like Jimmy? I mean, they're all into that shit, right?"

"You should go to the police," Jean said. "If your boyfriend is missing, you should report it. Also, you should press assault charges against Max. I'll be glad to act as a witness for you."

Blair looked more frightened than ever. "Are you shitting me or what? If I go to the cops, Max really will kill me. I've got little Andy to think of. Who's gonna take care of him if his mother ends up dead?"

"Okay, but for now we need to get you somewhere safe," Jean said. "Where Max can't find you."

Somewhere like right here, Jean thought.

Blair's battered face lost its fright amid of flood of confusion. "I still don't get it. Why are you doing this? Why are you helping us?"

"Like you said, Blair. Who's going to take care of Andy if you're dead?"

"I find it real hard to trust people," Blair said quietly.

"I hear you," Jean said. "I can tell you until I'm blue in the face that you can trust me. But it's meaningless. Put it this way, I'm going to do my best to protect you and Andy. How's that?"

Blair managed another smile. "I guess I don't have a whole lot of choice, do I?"

22

Jean put Blair in the guest bedroom with baby Andy asleep beside her. A couple of minutes later, Blair was out too.

Downstairs again in the kitchen, Jean drank a glass of tap water. She stood at the sink thinking and then went back up to her bedroom, applied a lot more make-up than she would ordinarily, changed into a tight skirt with a T-shirt, black knee-high boots, and a jade-colored leather jacket.

Finally, she dropped the Glock into her shoulder bag. All set.

For anything.

———————

It took Jean fifteen minutes to drive back out to the farm where she had encountered Max Flagg.

This time, she drove up the dirt road and parked in front of the farmhouse. A light still shone from inside and the front door remained open, the way she had left it when she had made her escape with Blair and the baby.

Inside, the air retained its rancid smell. From the kitchen, Jean heard a groan. Max Flagg lay curled on the floor more or less where she had dropped him.

There was blood from the laceration to his forehead where Jean had struck him with the iron.

Kneeling to him, Jean said, "Hey, you all right, fella?"

Max did not immediately respond. Then he groaned some more, shifting around on the floor. Jean felt some relief knowing she hadn't killed the guy.

Well, maybe not that much relief.

In the living room, amid the masses of laundry, she found clean towels and a facecloth. Back in the kitchen, she wet the facecloth under the tap in the sink and then managed to get Max into a sitting position and press the cloth against his forehead. After she cleaned the blood away, she saw that it wasn't as bad as she imagined. Still, it was nasty enough to debate if she should take the chance and get him to a hospital.

As if reading her mind, Max's eyes flickered and then opened, not so full of pain as suspicion. "Who are you?" he mumbled.

"Maybe your guardian angel," Jean replied.

"Bullshit," Max answered.

"I come in looking for Jimmy, and here you are, bleeding all over Jimmy's floor."

"Jimmy," Max groaned. "What the hell do you want with Jimmy?"

"What do you think? He called me earlier. Said to come over. What happened to him and that woman he's with?"

"Feel like shit," Max said by way of not answering the question.

"You should go to a hospital," Jean said. "Or I suppose being the good Samaritan I am, I should drive you to a hospital."

"I thought you were the goddamn guardian angel."

"Yeah, well, I guess I'm whatever you need me to be—maybe out of my effing mind."

"Can you help me up?"

"You sure you should move?"

"Gotta get up," he said.

He was so big that it was a struggle to get him off the floor and into a chair; big enough so that she allowed herself to marvel that she was able to beat him down in the first place. Finally in the chair, Max now held the face cloth against his forehead. When she removed it, she saw that the bleeding had pretty much stopped. She went to the sink, rinsed the cloth and then brought it back to him.

"Thanks," he said.

"How are you feeling?"

"Like shit," he said.

"What happened to you?"

"None of your goddamn business," he said, scowling, showing signs of the temper that allowed him to beat up a young woman while her baby lay in the other room.

"Aren't you the nicest guy," Jean said.

"Nothing nice about me, sweetheart," Max replied in a surly voice.

"Probably how you ended up bleeding all over the floor."

"That could have something to do with it," he admitted. Again, there was the flash of a smile; a bad guy with something resembling a sense of humor, Jean thought. Laugh-a-minute Max—until he killed you.

Max struggled to his feet, wobbled, and then grasped the edge of the chair to balance himself, dropping the facecloth. Blood dripped down his face. "Jesus Christ," he said.

"You're in no shape to do anything," Jean said.

"Gotta get out of here," he slurred, shaking his head, trying to clear it. He tried to stick his hand in his pocket, but it was too much for him. He sank back onto the chair. "Shit," he said, gasping.

"Let me," Jean said. "What are you looking for?"

"Cell phone," he said.

She reached into his pocket and pulled out the phone. He grabbed it out of her hand. "Hey," she said. "You're determined to be an asshole, aren't you?"

He didn't reply, placing the phone on the table beside him and then poking out a number. A voice came on the speaker: "Jesus, what time is it?"

Max snapped, "I'm at Jimmy's place. Come and get me."

"Everything all right?" the voice's initial irritation had been replaced by concern.

"Just get here as soon as you can."

Max swiped his phone shut and looked blearily at Jean. "I need you to get the hell out of here," he said.

"You're welcome," Jean said sarcastically. "Any time you need your ass saved, please give me a call."

Max's face darkened for an instant, then lightened again. "Hey, it's not that I don't appreciate what you did, okay? I'm a little shaky right now, that's all."

Jean stood. "Sure you're going to be all right?"

"Someone's coming. I'll be fine."

"Take care of yourself," Jean said. "And if I were you, in the future, I'd avoid whoever did this."

"Whoever did this is a dead man," Max pronounced.

"Tough guy, huh?" Jean said it with a tinge of sarcasm.

"The toughest," Max replied. There was no sarcasm.

"Well, good luck, tough guy." Jean started out of the room.

He called after her: "Hey." She stopped and turned to him. "What's your name, anyway?"

"Jean," she said.

"You a friend of Jimmy's?"

"I wouldn't go that far," Jean said. "Let's say we do business from time to time."

"I wouldn't worry about Jimmy," Max said.

"I never worry about Jimmy."

"I'm Max."

"Max who's bleeding again," Jean said. "Max who'd better get his ass to the hospital."

"Tell you what, Jean. I'll be in better shape tomorrow. Why don't you drop around to my office, say hello?"

"I've got better things to do than spend time saying hello to guys named Max."

"No, you don't. Believe me."

"No?"

"Dynamic Electric. On North Bronte. Come by. It'll be worth your precious time."

"Dynamic Electric? Don't tell me you're an electrician."

"Sure Jean," he said. "That's me. An electrician."

"Maybe I'll see you, Max, the electrician."

Jean ambled out the door.

———————

On the way back to her house, Jean tried not to think about what she had just done because what she had done was insane; walking straight back into the lion's den, nursing the asshole she had nearly killed with a well-placed iron. Max Flagg wasn't as close to death as she feared. Big, mean hombres like Max Flagg did not kill so easily. A lesson for the future she would do well to keep in mind, she told herself.

Max would survive, but could she? That was the insane part. Now that she was on his radar, it would be difficult to simply disappear. She must play this out but play it out how? And what was she to do with the mother and child currently sound asleep in the guest bedroom?

All this could be dealt with in the morning, she concluded as she came into the kitchen. Right now, all she wanted to do was fall into bed and get a good night's sleep. She poured herself a glass of water and then stood at the counter drinking it. That's when she noticed her wallet on the floor.

She had left so quickly she had neglected to take it with her. Still, she hadn't left it on the floor. She bent down and scooped it up. The wallet had contained about one hundred dollars in cash.

The money was gone.

She tossed the wallet on the kitchen table and went upstairs.

As she figured it would be, the guest bedroom was empty.

Except for the sleeping baby.

23

Peter did not expect to find Amy Wu-Chan in his living room. Professional in a dark business suit, a minimum of jewelry, smelling great, the way she always did.

He was somewhat irritated that she had arrived un-announced. Already, he was beginning to regret having given her a key to his place. He liked her, wanted to have sex with her, believed he could manipulate her to his own political ends but he didn't like her showing up whenever she felt like it.

If he had thought she was there for sex, that notion evaporated when he tried to kiss her. She ducked away, saying, "Sorry, I can't start anything."

"Can't?" For some reason, Peter found this amusing. *Can't?*

"This is business," she stated. No affection when business was concerned, Peter supposed.

Straightening, he backed off a few paces, working up a smile. "I'm always willing to do business," he said. "Business it is. Would you like a drink?"

"I'm fine, thanks," Amy said.

"If this is business, I'm probably going to need a drink. Let me get something."

"Please, sit down so we can get this out of the way. I've got another meeting in an hour or so."

Wordlessly, Peter arranged himself on the sofa, taking care to position himself in such a way as to look interested but at the same time relaxed—although, abruptly, he was anything but.

"Where are we with the Milton situation?" Amy's tone was clipped and professional.

"We are in a good place," Peter replied. "I expect The Fairground proposal will come before the full council in the next couple of weeks. At that point, I anticipate our plan will be approved and then we can get to work."

"All right, that is good news, except the premier got a phone call from Milton's acting mayor Bal yesterday. He made it quite clear to her that he is vehemently opposed to the development and will do everything in his power to ensure it never happens."

"That's not the case," Peter said smoothly.

Amy's expression remained neutral except for an almost imperceptible raising of her tailored eyebrows. "It isn't? Then what is?"

"The mayor will agree to the development," Peter stated flatly.

"Then why would he tell the premier otherwise?"

"There may be certain things he feels he has to say for public consumption. Privately, he holds another view."

"Does he?"

The acting mayor will agree to the development. Trust me, Amy. It will happen."

"I've trusted you until now," Amy said.

"You slept with me," Peter said. "I'm not so sure that's the same as trust."

"And here I thought it was," Amy said.

"Let's not confuse the two," Peter said.

Amy tried not to but she looked wounded and for the first time since he got home, Peter felt as though he had regained control.

"You really are a bastard," Amy said.

"I am. That's why I will get this done. No matter what gets in the way, I will get this done."

"Even if it's the acting mayor."

"I will get it done," Peter said.

Amy looked somewhat reassured. "As long as you're sure about this, Peter. We are way past the time for bullshit."

"As it happens, I'm meeting with the mayor tomorrow to firm up the details of his support."

Amy slowly rose to her feet, fighting against the uncertainty she still felt. "I'll report what you've told me back to the premier."

"Please do," Peter said. He rose to face her. "Are you sure you can't stay?"

"It's just fucking, isn't it?"

"Come on, don't be sore," Peter said. "You know what I mean."

"I suppose I do. I probably knew from the beginning. It's just that every once in a while, you forget things you shouldn't forget."

"Look, I'm not trying to be any more difficult than necessary. I'm only trying to get this project off the ground. The premier's support is invaluable. I'm don't want to do anything that jeopardizes that."

"No?"

"Not unless I have to."

"Then this ends with a threat, is that it?"

"I don't think threats are necessary. Do you?"

"What time are you meeting with the acting mayor?" Amy asked.

"Three o'clock," Peter said.

"When the meeting's over, please phone and update me."

"As soon as it's finished."

"That's it, then." Amy swirled away. The last thing she saw as she exited was Peter on the sofa.

Staring straight ahead.

––––––––––

Eve had warned her that certain subjects should never be discussed at Queen's Park no matter what. So, Amy went directly home, poured herself a drink and waited.

An hour later, Eve arrived, looking peeved. "I thought you were coming back to the office," she said in a tight voice.

"I thought it best to wait until you got home before filling you in," Amy said.

Eve put her brief case down. She looked tired. "Fill me in on what?" she asked.

"Late this afternoon I met with Peter Earp," Amy said.

"The duplicitous bastard, Peter Earp," Eve stated. "Did you sleep with him again?"

"I think he was surprised that I didn't."

"That makes two of us," Eve said. "How many times have you fucked him?"

"Hundreds," Amy said. "I've lost count."

"I hate you," Eve said.

Amy laughed and then came over and joined Eve on the sofa. The best thing when her lover was in one of her jealous snits was to ignore the jealous snit.

"For what it's worth, Peter says Amar Bal is onside, that he will vote in favor of the fairground development and that the council will back him."

"That's not what Bal told me," Eve said. "Your lover is not telling the truth."

"He's not my lover," Amy said. "Not anymore."

"No?" Eve didn't bother to hide her expression of relief.

Amy gently took Eve's hand. "Let's give him the benefit of the doubt, at least for the time being. Knowing Peter, he's pulling a rabbit out of his hat that no one expects. I don't know how he's going to do it, I don't want to know. But I suspect he's going to do it."

"I don't like any of this," Eve said.

"If you've taught me anything this last couple of years, it's that there are times when we end up having to do the things we don't like before we do the things we do. If I'm not mistaken this is one of those times."

"I also taught you never to get into shit you can't get out of," Eve said. "I'm afraid I may have ignored my own rule with this bastard."

"You'll get through this," Amy said. "You always do."

"I was hoping I'd taught you something else."

"What's that?"

"How to love," Eve said.

"That was an easy lesson to learn," Amy said.

She drew Eve to her.

24

Hikers discovered the body in a hollow at the edge of a wooded area a few miles south of Georgetown.

No one, Mickey Dann reflected, any longer dropped a body south of the city, there being too much development, not enough remote areas left where a corpse could lie safely undiscovered for who knew how long. It was a matter of luck that the trio of hikers stumbled across the body. Otherwise, it might never have been found.

Three fit guys in their mid-forties, outfitted in the latest MEC hiking gear stood off to the side being interviewed by uniformed officers, distracted by the all the police activity swirling around.

Someone had shot the corpse in the back of his head so most of the skull was gone.

Doc Prescott stood at the crest of the hollow scribbling into a small notebook as Mickey and Petrusiak approached. "What do you think, Doc?" Petrusiak asked. "Dead about a week?"

Doc grimaced a bit as he continued to write. "Big-time Toronto detective," he said. "What? You taking over my job now?"

"No way, Doc. Tell me I'm wrong."

Doc Prescott stopped writing and sighed. "In this case, friend Petrusiak, you are probably right. Putrefaction has long since set in. You can see by the green discoloration of the body's skin, the bloating that has taken place. How quickly this happens depends on the temperature. It's been fairly cool lately so that slows things down. Thus, I'd say a week."

He snapped his notebook closed. "I'll leave you gentlemen to it. I'm going back to Milton to turn in my resignation." He gave Petrusiak a sideways look. "I'll be recommending this prick as my replacement."

Doc Prescott wandered off.

"You sure know how to make friends, Glen," Mickey observed dryly.

"To hell with him," Petrusiak said. "He's a goddamn dinosaur, anyway."

"A dinosaur who still knows what he's doing."

"Let's see what we've got here." Petrusiak knelt to more closely inspect the body. He wrinkled his nose and then said, "I thought so. It's Jimmy Boyd."

Mickey looked at his partner, impressed despite himself. "You know him?"

"Low-level creep and drug dealer I arrested in Toronto a few years ago. If he's not in jail, he's on his way there."

"No jails around here," Mickey said.

Well, they could have offed him in Toronto and then brought out here. Why would you go to all this trouble for a shithead like Jimmy?"

"A drug guy shot to death in the Halton region."

"Petrusiak got to his feet. "That sound like anyone we know?"

Mickey said, "I don't think the world is short an electrician today."

"We could ask Max Flagg if he is missing an employee."

"Be nice if we could put this on Max and get that asshole off the streets," Mickey said.

"Let's go talk to him," Petrusiak said.

At first, she didn't recognize the sound.

Then she realized what it was: a baby crying.

Good god, she thought. A *baby*. The events of the previous evening flooded back.

Jean bolted into an upright position. Baby Andy squirmed beside her. He wasn't crying so much as making contented sounds, a newcomer to the world and happy to be here. Jean swept him into her arms. Andy wiggled fat little fingers at her, his big eyes alive, his mouth curling into a welcoming smile.

"Don't do this to me," Jean said to him. "Don't allow me to fall for you, little guy. I hate to tell you this because you're happy today but given your circumstances, a shitty life awaits."

Andy merely gurgled more and delivered another heart-stopping smile. Shit, Jean thought. The little bugger lit up the world.

At least he lit hers this morning. What the hell was she going to do? Well, judging from the odor releasing from him, a diaper change should be the immediate order of business.

Carrying Andy downstairs, Jean got a towel, placed him on the kitchen counter, cleaned him up, changed his diaper with a lot more alacrity than she would have given herself credit for, fed him his bottle, dressed him in the jeans and striped T-shirt she had bought the night before.

He didn't start to cry until she set him in his car seat.

Jean gave him a cross look. "Why are you crying? There's no reason to cry, okay? Therefore, don't cry."

Andy wasn't listening. He continued to wail.

Jean picked him up. Immediately, Andy stopped crying and began making more of the happy gurgling sounds that were quickly becoming his trademark. "What am I going to do with you?" Jean asked as she held him.

Andy smiled. Jean's heart melted.

She carried him back to the counter, balancing him in one arm while she struggled to make herself morning coffee. Once that was accomplished, she sat with him at the kitchen table, sipping her coffee while Andy snuggled against her.

Contentedly snuggled. Good god, she thought. She was enjoying this.

What was wrong with her, anyway? She gazed down at Andy thinking there was another possibility, one she rarely encountered these days: maybe nothing was wrong.

This was absolutely right.

25

Andy was in his car seat as Jean drove to Bronte Street North and parked across the street from Dynamic Electric. As usual, the concrete pillbox beyond the chain-link fence looked deserted.

She carried Andy inside the building. No one was behind the counter. She called out, "Hello? Anybody here?"

A voice replied: "In the back."

She rounded the counter and went through an open doorway. A narrow hallway ended at a small, cluttered office with a battered metal desk and a sofa against the wall. Max Flagg, looking the worse for wear, lay on the sofa. The side of his face where Jean had hit him with the iron was so swollen and purple his right eye was sealed shut. He was all set to play the title role in *The Elephant Man*, Jean thought. A bandage covered his forehead. If Jean was concerned that her visit might have caused him to become violent, she needn't have worried. In his present state, Max was not about to move, let alone hurt anyone.

His one good eye gave her a baleful look. "What the hell you doing with that kid?"

"Raising him to become prime minister of Canada."

Max managed the semblance of a smile. "Don't make me laugh. It's too goddamn painful."

"I like you in pain, Max. It suits you."

"Jean, right?"

"That's right, Max. We met when I saved your ass."

"Saved my ass, shit. Anyone ever tell you, you're a bitch?"

"All the time. That's why I carry this kid around with me. Softens my personality."

Max winced as he smiled again. "Okay, what's up? What are you doing here?"

"What do you mean? You're the one who told me to drop around."

"Yeah, I guess I did."

"Besides, I'm still looking for Jimmy."

At that mention of Jimmy's name, Max's smile evaporated. "I wouldn't worry about Jimmy."

"No? Why wouldn't I?"

"Jimmy's a loser. You're not a loser, are you?"

"Maybe he's the love of my life."

"No way," Max replied firmly. "He's the loser of your life, not the love."

"What are you getting at?"

"Who says I'm getting at anything?"

"If you're not, then I'm wasting my time, aren't I?"

"Are you?"

"Game time is over," Jean said, "I thought I was coming to the right place. I guess not. I'm taking my kid and going home."

"Hold on," Max said. "Cool your jets. Sit down a minute."

"What have you got in mind?" Jean remained standing.

"Irma, bitch who was working for me, just walked out. No loss. But maybe you're different."

"Yeah, I don't like being called a bitch."

"Could be that I could use someone like you," Max said. "I've got a bunch of macho assholes working for me. All brawn, no brains."

"I don't know the first thing about electricity," Jean said.

"It happens when you flip a light switch," Max replied. "That's all you need to know."

"I figured it might be something like that."

"Except I don't need an electrician."

"No? Then what do you need?"

"Someone kickass. Someone like yourself."

"To do what?"

"To do what it takes."

"Sure, I could handle that," Jean said.

"Tell you what," Max said. "You got a cell phone?"

"Sure," Jean said. "Who doesn't?"

"Give me your number."

"Why would I do that?"

"I might want to get in touch with you."

"What for?"

"Just give me your number, Jean."

Jean gave him a number which he thumbed into the phone as she picked up the baby seat.

"We do something," Max said, "I don't want you bringing the kid, okay?"

"That's fine. I'll give him up for adoption."

Max couldn't resist another wince-inducing smile. "You really are a badass."

"The baddest," Jean said.

She went out the door, sensing rather than seeing Max's admiring gaze.

———————

"We go in there, we brace him," Mickey Dann said.

"Premature, you ask me," said Petrusiak.

"You know Glen, I'm beginning to get tired of you wanting to zag every time I suggest we zig."

"You think that's what I'm doing?"

"Yeah, I do."

Petrusiak threw up his hands. "Okay, the hell with it, let's go in there and talk to him."

"That's more like it," Mickey said.

"I still say it's premature," Petrusiak said.

Mickey rolled his eyes as he started out of the car. He stopped abruptly when he saw who was exiting Dynamic Electric.

Petrusiak said, "Shit, is that who I think it is?"

"Who do you think it is?"

"It's goddamn Jean Whitlock."

"With a baby," Mickey said, his voice full of wonder.

"What the hell is she doing in there and what the hell is she doing with a baby?" Petrusiak threw a glance at Mickey.

"Don't look at me," Mickey said.

26

Gee, Max, what happened to you?" Glen Petrusiak said as soon as he and Mickey were inside Max Flagg's office.

Max stirred on the sofa and that caused him to grunt with pain. "Cops." He managed to say.

"Good guess," said Petrusiak, flashing his badge.

"What do you assholes want?" Max demanded.

"You know, Max," Mickey said, "it does my heart good to see the prick who has beat the shit out of so many citizens in the Halton district finally gets the shit kicked out of him. Can you give us his name? Glen and I would like to pin a medal on him."

"I ran into a door. By the way, I don't have to talk to you pricks."

"Yes, you do, Max," Mickey said, settling into the chair in front of the desk while Petrusiak remained standing.

"The thing is, Max," Petrusiak went on. "We can have a pleasant chat here in your office or we can arrest you and haul you over to police headquarters. I can promise you that won't be nearly so pleasant."

Max hesitated for a time before he said, "Always glad to cooperate with members of law enforcement. What can I do for you?"

"Let's talk about Jimmy Boyd," Mickey said.

"Never heard of him," Max promptly replied.

"That's funny," Petrusiak said. "We heard he works for you."

"You heard wrong," Max said.

"Now, as crazy as it seems, Max, we might find out you are lying to us. If that's the case, it would not go well for you, to say the least."

"What? Lying to cops is a crime?"

"Lying to us is," Mickey said. The edge in his voice had replaced the previous friendly tone.

"He might have worked for me," Max amended. "I'll have to check my employment records. What difference does it make, anyway?"

"It wouldn't make any difference," Mickey said. "Except for the fact that we were just with Jimmy in a field north of the city, near Georgetown."

"Georgetown?" Max shook his head. "What's Jimmy doing up there?"

"Hard to say," Petrusiak answered. "Jimmy wasn't communicative."

"If I remember correctly, Jimmy doesn't talk much."

"Difficult for him to talk with half his head blown off."

"That's too bad." Max sounded as though it wasn't all that bad.

"You wouldn't know who would want to kill Jimmy, would you, Max?" Mickey asked.

"Like I say, I barely knew the guy."

"Any chance you would have killed him, Max?"

Max forced a smile. "Now why would I go and do something like that?"

"Because that's what you do to people you don't like," said Mickey. "Could that be a good enough reason?"

"Look at me. I can hardly sit up. Do I look like I'm able to kill anyone?"

"What are you trying to tell us, Max?" Mickey asked. "Are you trying to tell us you didn't run into a door?"

"Let's say I was mugged."

"Big mean bastard like yourself?"

"They snuck up on me from behind."

"When did this happen?"

"A while ago. Can't remember."

"You can't remember when someone beat the shit out of you?"

"Hey, you should see the other guy."

"The other guy wouldn't have been Jimmy Boyd?" Mickey asked. "Did he beat you up?"

"Give me a break. Jimmy couldn't beat up shit."

"Then who?"

"Persons unknown," Max said mildly.

Petrusiak asked, "What about a woman, Max? You got a girlfriend?"

"Lots of girlfriends," Max said. "Ladies, no matter what they say, they still like 'em big and mean. You might say I'm a babe magnet."

"What about that woman who just left?" Petrusiak asked.

"What about her?"

"Does she like 'em big and mean?"

"I imagine she does," Max said.

"Is she one of your girlfriends?"

Max smirked and said, "Not yet. I'm working on it."

Mickey and Petrusiak traded glances.

"Jimmy has a wife and child, did you know that?" asked Mickey.

"I keep saying, I don't know Jimmy. How could I know anything about his marital situation?"

"We can't seem to find them," Petrusiak said.

"Look around to your heart's content, you're not gonna find any wives and kids."

"This isn't going away," Mickey said, leaning into Max. "There's a murdered man and a missing woman and a baby. That raises the level bigtime so if you got anything to tell us, tell us now while there is still a chance of you getting out of this. Otherwise—"

"Otherwise, it's a damned good thing I'm innocent."

Mickey stood up and said, "You're a lot of things, Max. Innocent isn't one of them."

"Don't tell my mother," Max said.

27

"What the hell was that all about?" Petrusiak asked as he and Mickey headed back to their car.

"That was Max Flagg denying he killed Jimmy Boyd while at the same time pretty much convincing me that he *did* kill Jimmy."

"I'm talking about Jean Whitlock as Max's new girlfriend."

"He didn't say she was his new girlfriend," Mickey amended.

"He said he was working on it. We see her walking out of there—with a baby, for God's sake. I repeat, what's going on?"

"I have no idea," Mickey said as they reached their car.

"We need to have another talk with her," Petrusiak said.

"What would it be? The follow-up to your accusations that she hung her uncle from a lamppost?"

"Then you tell me what we should do."

"Let me handle it."

"The jealous ex-boyfriend," Petrusiak said.

"I'm not jealous and I'm not an ex-boyfriend."

"Then what are you?"

"I'm working on it," Mickey said.

As he got behind the wheel, Mickey thought, What the hell is she up to? Why would Jean be mixed up with a lowlife like Max Flagg? They didn't come much scummier than Max. He couldn't believe she would have anything to do with him. But there she was coming out of his office.

With a baby, no less.

What the hell *was* she up to?

———————

What the *hell* was she doing? Jean thought as she parked her car.

Oh, yeah, working for Peter Earp. Right. Somehow, that involved beating up Max Flagg, caring for someone else's baby and landing a job with the town's worst crook.

All within the last twenty-four hours or so.

What the hell was she doing?

Andy started to make noises, not crying exactly, gentle sounds of a baby in need of attention. Jean got out of the car and reached into the back to unbuckle the seatbelt holding in the baby seat. "What's the matter, little guy?" she asked as she pulled the car seat out. "Not getting enough attention? You may need that diaper changed again. Or are you hungry?"

Andy merely gurgled in reply.

"Okay, a bit of both by the sound of things."

And on top of everything else, she thought, here I am talking to a baby.

And enjoying it.

When she opened the front door, immediately there was an all-too-familiar vibe. Someone had broken in again.

Obviously, her shitty locks weren't stopping anybody who wanted in. The question was, who was doing this, and what were they looking for? Whatever it was presumably had not shown up in Jock Whitlock's previously pilfered files.

In the kitchen, she changed Andy's diaper and fed him his formula. He sucked happily on his bottle and then fell asleep. His little head cocked to one side looking as cute as a bug's ear, she thought, smiling despite herself.

Smiling in the face of all the shit raining down around her. Smiling knowing she was determined to care for and protect this helpless little boy. Smiling because this was the last thing in the world she ever expected to smile about.

The phone rang. When Jean swiped it open, a voice said, "Is he all right?"

"Blair?"

"Tell me Andy is okay."

"Andy is fine. Where are you?"

"Look, I'm sorry I ran off like that, okay? But if he finds me, he's going to kill me."

"Come back here. I will protect you. The police, too."

"I'm sorry about Andy, I really am," Blair said tearfully. "I just don't know what else to do, I don't."

"Blair—"

"Take care of him, please. Protect him. You can do that. Right now, I can't."

"I can protect you, too—"

But she was gone.

"Goddamn, you!" Jean exclaimed to the phone, a metallic object that could care less what she said, could care less that she was left with a stranger's baby, could care less that it was now occurring to Jean that this might not be a temporary arrangement, Jean playing the good Samaritan, knowing the role would soon end.

Maybe—and this freaked her out—it wasn't going to end.

The knock on the door caused her to freeze. Given current circumstances and the time of the night, a door knock was not a good thing, particularly since she was in the kitchen with a sleeping baby that was not hers. She had no inclination to answer questions about how this state of affairs came to be.

Picking up the baby seat, she hurried upstairs to set the seat on the floor beside the bed. She stood over Andy for a couple of moments to see if he awakened. The little guy slept on.

More knocking. Jean went back downstairs to the front door. When she opened it, Mickey Dann said, "Hey."

"Hey yourself," Jean replied.

"Can I come in?"

"Is this an official visit? Or are you just dropping by to say hello?"

"A little of both," Mickey said.

Jean thought of sleeping Andy upstairs, praying sleeping Andy would stay that way.

"Is everything all right?" Mickey asked, reacting to her hesitation.

She opened the door wider. "It's late, that's all."

"I can come back," Mickey offered.

"No, it's all right. Come in."

He stepped inside, immediately noticing the mess of the house. Jean kicked herself. She had been so busy with Andy, she had forgotten about the disorder of the house.

"What happened here?" he asked. "Looks like…"

"What?"

"I was going to say it looks like a tornado blew through but really it looks as though someone broke in."

"Good detective work," Jean said.

"You aren't going to phone police?"

"I just got home," Jean said.

"From your visit to Dynamic Electric." It was not a question.

Jean gave him a look. "You're not following me, are you?"

"Why would I follow you, Jean?"

"I don't know. You can't live without me?"

"That possibility aside, it has more to do with Jimmy Boyd."

"Jimmy Boyd? What about him?"

"You know Jimmy?"

"How should I know him?"

"We found him lying in a field south of George-town."

"And Petrusiak thinks I knocked him off, too. Is that it"

"Jimmy worked for Dynamic Electric. We went around to talk to his boss, a lowlife scumbag named Max Flagg."

"And you saw me."

"And we saw you."

"Okay."

"That's your cue to tell me what you were doing there."

"Not that it's any of your business but I was trying to hire someone to update the wiring in this house," Jean said.

"Max thinks you're his new girlfriend."

"Whatever happens between Max and me, first of all, he has to fix the wiring," Jean said.

Mickey gave her a look and then said, "What about the baby?"

"What baby?" Jean, all innocence.

"The baby you were carrying out of Dynamic Electric."

"I have no idea what you're talking about," Jean said.

"Yes, you do. We saw you leave. You were carrying a baby."

"You're delusional."

"Am I?"

Mickey would have said more except he was inter-rupted by the sound of a baby crying.

28

"Did you know that seventy-five per cent of the world's corporate profits are held in only four tax havens?"

Acting Mayor Amar Bal looked relaxed as he sat at his desk in the mayor's office but his words were edged with righteous anger.

"This is a disgrace," he added.

Peter tried not allow his eyes to glaze over as he sat across from the mayor listening to this nonsense.

"There is no accountability," the acting mayor continued. "The rich live everywhere, do business everywhere, but they pay taxes nowhere. It is left to the world's poor to pay, to keep the roads open that the rich drive on, to maintain the waterways the rich boat on, to provide the services the rich count on."

"No question there is a great deal of financial disparity," Peter said, struggling to sound as though he cared when he really didn't, thinking that this was the way of the world, always had been. Sitting in Milton, Amar Bal and Peter Earp were not going to change that.

It had been difficult getting this meeting in the first place and now the price he had to pay was listening to Amar babble on about the shortcomings of the rich.

Peter would have preferred to have the meeting on neutral ground, but Amar would have none of it. Fifteen minutes, no more, and in his office.

Tamara, his sister, was an uncomfortable presence beside him. Peter didn't like that given what he might have to do, but he had little choice. Time was running out. He had to keep moving. He had to produce results or deal with an unhappy father-in-law. The unhappiness of John Pesce was not something he wanted to face.

He swallowed hard, trying to keep down his rising sense of panic.

"What about you, Mr. Earp, where is your company located?" Amar said, his gaze abruptly riveted on Peter.

"Well, we're here in Milton and in Toronto."

"No, but where do you pay taxes?"

"Well, we pay taxes in Canada like any other Canadian company," Peter explained, silently praying they could soon get past this crap.

"But where is your corporate headquarters?"

Peter shifted in his chair before he said, "We have a number of companies, some of them headquartered in the Cayman Islands."

"A tax shelter," Amar pronounced.

"Everything we do is legal," Peter said in his best reassuring voice. "We pay all the taxes that are required by law. I would like to point out that, unlike a lot of financial people, we provide something tangible and real, places for people to live. We add value to people's lives."

"While avoiding paying taxes," Amar shot back.

Peter shook his head. "That's not true. If you approve our application to develop The Fairground as a townhouse community, not only will it add substantially to the town's tax base but it will also add much-needed population density to a downtown that otherwise is about to die. That's not taking our profits offshore, Mr. Mayor, that's making a contribution to the life of this community."

"I'm sorry, I don't believe it," Amar stated. "You well know my position, Mr. Earp. I'm surprised that we are still having this conversation."

"We are having this conversation because the town needs this development and right now you are the only person standing in the way of making that happen."

"Good," said Amar. "That is what I want."

"You see, that's where you are wrong. You do want it to happen."

Amar gave a quizzical look "How is that possible, Mr. Earp?"

"Because if you don't approve The Fairground, then, I'm afraid, things could get nasty. I'm sure you don't want that, Mr. Mayor"

Amar's placid features had rearranged into an unpleasant scowl. "And why should my objection to your terrible scheme make anything 'nasty' as you say?"

"Because I gave Tamara ten thousand dollars to influence your vote."

Peter didn't look at her as he said this but from the sound of Tamara's gasp he knew he had hit home. He added: "I don't believe you would want that information to get out to the public, Mr. Mayor."

Amar looked as though someone had slapped him. "But that is not true," he said in a high-pitched voice. "You are lying."

"I'm afraid I'm not lying," Peter responded calmly. "You may or may not be aware of your sister's gambling problem. She owes quite a bit of money. I've helped her satisfy that debt."

Amar turned his gaze on his sister "Tamara, is any of this true?"

"Oh, God," she said amid a sudden torrent of tears, turning to Peter, trembling. "What are you doing? What are you doing?" She buried her head in her hands and cried some more.

"I'm sorry, I don't want any of this," Peter said. He addressed Tamara, speaking in as sincere a voice as he could muster. "I like you. I truly do. But I'm afraid your brother has put me in a position where I have no choice."

She raised her head to him, tears streaming down her face. "You bastard," she said quietly. "You terrible, awful bastard."

Amar's face had become ashen. He sat rigidly in his chair saying nothing. Tamara continued to cry as Peter stood.

"Nothing of what we have talked about today has to go further than this room," he said, speaking directly to Amar. "Obviously, I've as much invested in silence as you have. That's why I've done this the way I have. If this becomes public, we are all ruined. If it doesn't, then we can all go on with our lives in a community that, although you may not think so, will be better off with this development."

He paused before he added, "I'll be looking forward to a positive response when it comes to a vote at town council, Mr. Mayor."

"*Acting* mayor," Amar Bal snapped.

————————

Peter came outside, taking deep breaths, feeling suddenly dizzy and unbalanced. That was better, he thought. Take it easy. It was over. He had accomplished what he had set out to accomplish. The development would go through, he was certain of that.

As he started toward his car, his cell phone sounded. He swiped it open and Amy Wu-Chan said, "How did it go?"

His head was clearing a bit now, he wasn't feeling quite so nauseous. He took another breath and said, "It went fine."

"What does that mean?" Amy demanded.

"He will vote in favor of the project."

"He said that?"

"In so many words, yes."

"In so many words? That doesn't sound like yes to me."

"There are things you don't have to know. Trust me. It will go through." The conversation was making Peter dizzy again. This was too much. He shouldn't be doing this. Too goddamn much.

Amy's voice was coming at him from somewhere in the distance. "We're counting on you," he dimly heard her say.

"Yes," he said.

A park bench was nearby. He slumped down on it. Not feeling well at all.

"Peter?" he heard her say.

"I'm here."

"Are you all right?"

"Fine," he said. "It's done. Let's move on."

"Will I see you tonight?"

"Not tonight," he said. God, he thought, the last thing he needed was the necessity of dealing with her.

"That's fine, I'll talk to you later," Amy said brusquely and then hung up.

He put his cell phone away and stood, still feeling woozy. The sun was hot and bright in his eyes. He squinted into it, taking more deep breaths. A blurry figure blocked the sunlight. He shook his head, trying to clear his vision.

He saw Tamara Bal coming toward him, her face tense and tear-stained.

Tamara stopped, crying out something he didn't quite catch. He couldn't hear anything except the rush of air.

Then he heard something like a far-off explosion. There was what felt like a hard blow to his chest and the next thing he was falling back.

He hit the ground, his body filling with pain. He thought he saw Tamara looming over him.

There were two more distant explosions.

And then there was nothing.

29

As soon as Jean picked up Andy and carried him downstairs, he quietened and began to make his now familiar happy gurgling sounds. It was amazing, really. As soon as the child was shown the least bit of affection he was transformed into Perfect Baby, camera-ready for the label on a pouch of Gerber baby food.

"I'm only baby-sitting him," Jean said as she entered the living room to confront a skeptical-looking Mickey Dann. "Cute, huh?"

"Aren't all babies cute?" Mickey asked bending to get a closer look. Andy reached out and pulled Mickey's nose.

"See? He's irresistible," Jean said.

Mickey straightened up. "Yeah, I guess so," he said, not sounding convinced. "Whose kid is it, anyway?"

"A friend," Jean said vaguely.

"Does this friend have a name?"

"Just a friend," Jean said. "This has been a difficult adjustment for her. She doesn't want a lot of attention right now. I'm trying to help out."

"The seasoned mother that you are," Mickey said.

"Hey, give me a break, I'm beginning to get the hang of it," she said, jiggling Andy a bit and getting a smile out of him. "And this little guy is such a pleasure, being a mother isn't so hard at all."

"Why you even take him to visit our local crime boss," Mickey said.

"Like I told you, I need some electrical work done, that's all."

"That's your story. But you know what? I'm having trouble believing you."

"I seem to have a hard time convincing you and Petrusiak of anything. He thinks I killed my uncle. You believe I am sleeping with known criminals."

"Let's not forget Glen's suspicion that you might be involved in the murder of Jimmy Boyd."

"Whom I've never met. But don't let that stop you."

"The point is, Jean, you're not telling me everything," Mickey said.

"You always say that."

"And I'm usually right." He looked around, indicating the mess of the house. "A case in point."

"I told you. Someone broke in."

"Which you never reported."

"I repeat, I just got home. I'm being grilled by a local detective. I haven't had a spare moment."

"What's missing?"

"As far as I can see right now, it doesn't look as though anything was taken."

"Then why do you suppose someone broke in here?"

Jean thought she had better tell Mickey something that at least came close to the truth. She said, "All right, this is the second break-in. The first time, I had just been given boxes of files from my uncle's office. Whoever got in here, took the boxes."

"Okay, but what about this time?"

"I imagine they didn't find what they were looking for and so they came back for a second look."

"Do you have any idea what they are looking for?"

"I went through most of the boxes. They were full of old bills, copies of council minutes, newspaper clippings. Nothing important. Nothing you would want to steal."

"Why didn't you call the police?"

"Because right now I don't want my life any more complicated than it already is."

"What with a baby to raise and everything."

"I'm *not* raising, Andy," Jean protested. "I'm babysitting him, that's all."

"For a nameless friend."

"That's right."

"I'll say it again: you're not being honest with me."

"I'm being as honest as I can be."

"That's called lying, Jean."

Andy began struggling in her arms and making noises that weren't as happy as before and that saved her from having to respond to Mickey.

"This guy needs attention," she said.

Mickey looked disappointed. "I hope you know what you're doing."

"Surprisingly, it turns out I know more than I thought I did when it comes to changing a diaper."

"That isn't what I meant."

Again, she was saved from a response—something along the lines of "I know what I'm doing," when it was just the opposite—by Mickey's phone.

"Yeah?" he said into the phone. He paused for a time and then said, "All right, I'll be there in a couple of minutes."

He put his phone away. "Gotta go."

"Everything all right?"

"Apparently the acting mayor's sister just shot someone in front of the Town Hall."

————

When Amy entered the premier's office, the Red Queen was finishing a meeting with Charlie Whelan, the cowboy hat-wearing minister of agriculture. Amy thought the cows on Charlie's Western Ontario farm outside St. Thomas had more brains than he did.

Eve shook Charlie's hand, telling him they would be in touch, the catch-all phrase, meaningless but it served as an efficient way to usher visitors out of her office. She would not in all probability be in touch but that didn't matter. Still, even if he was dumber than his cows, Charlie had the country smarts enough to know a brushoff when he saw one. He leaned into the premier, his gravelly voice conspiratorial.

"Madam, I don't have to remind you about plummeting poll numbers and a whole bunch of voters that are pretty pissed at this government."

"No, Charlie," Eve said. "You don't have to remind me."

"Want you to know I'm on your side, okay? Me and my constituents are in need of a little back-scratching, that's all."

"I understand, Charlie." There was an edge to the patience in Eve's voice.

"Then madam, I will leave you to it." He doffed his hat and used it to execute a sweeping bow before making his exit. Eve rolled her eyes and slumped against her desk. "Jesus Christ," she said.

"Are you all right?" Amy with the concern showing in her voice.

"Other than the fact that my own party, led by the country bumpkin Charlie Whelan, is ready to cut off my head in front of a crowd on Queen's Park Crescent, I'm fine."

Eve sighed again when she saw Amy's grim look. "Don't tell me. More bad news."

"I don't have all the details as yet, but there's been a shooting in Milton."

"What about it?"

"The mayor's sister."

"Tamara Bal? She's been shot?" Eve looked alarmed.

"No, she apparently did the shooting."

"Tamara shot someone?"

"That's what I'm hearing," Amy said.

"Who did she shoot?"

"I don't have that information yet."

A cold involuntary shiver shook Eve's body. "Jesus Christ. Wasn't Peter Earp meeting with the mayor this afternoon—Tamara's brother?"

"I hope I'm wrong, but, yes."

Eve closed her eyes for a moment and then breathed, "Good God in heaven."

"I'm not saying that's necessarily the case," Amy hurriedly added. "But I am saying it's a possibility we should prepare for."

Eve managed to steady her breathing. "Let's hope it isn't," she said.

"But in case it is…"

"We're screwed. The development will never go through. What's more, if they start digging into Peter's involvement, my name is bound to come up. Christ knows where that's going to lead."

"I think we can weather any storm that comes out of this," Amy said.

"You do, do you? Well, if you'd just spent the past hour with Charlie Whelan, you might have second thoughts about that."

"I've got some ideas," Amy said. "But right now, let's not yell before we are hurt."

"Don't tell me. Your mother used to say that to you."

"As a matter of fact, she did," Amy said. "First of all, let's be certain it is Peter and then find out whether he's dead or has just wounded."

Amy moved to embrace her lover. Eve shot out a staying hand. "Don't. Not here. Never here."

Amy stopped dead, and then moved back. "Sorry," she said.

"Get on the phone," Eve ordered. "Get me more information."

30

Jean spent an hour or so fussing with Andy, enjoying the pleasurable business of bathing him, dressing him, getting him fed, keeping him entertained. When he was tired, she lay him down and sat with him until he fell to sleep.

Thinking again how—what?—satisfying? Was that the word? Yes, it was. How satisfying were these simple routines. Ordinary life, the life she did not know. The life she—no, it wasn't possible—yearned for?

Not that. She had never wanted ordinary and yet here it was and she was loving it.

There must be something wrong with her. Or maybe this wasn't so wrong after all.

With Andy settled, she went to work cleaning up the mess left by the intruders. This time, the devastation was much worse than she initially had observed. Pot lights had been torn out of the ceilings, the bottom ripped out of the sofa and two easy chairs. Upstairs, the mattress in her bedroom had been yanked off the bed and cut open, its insides strewn about. Shelves had been torn out of the closets. The medicine cabinet in the bathroom had been pried off the wall and left on the floor.

Despite the destruction, Jean couldn't see that anything had been taken. The intruders had searched with increasing desperation for something they could not find. But what was it? They had all Jock's files, didn't they?

Well, they presumably didn't think so, otherwise they wouldn't have taken the chance breaking in again and tearing the place apart.

Then she thought of the one thing they didn't get.

The key.

They hadn't found that. She had hidden it behind a loose brick in the downstairs wall behind a pair of plastic bins filled with hoses and sprinklers.

It was still there.

———————

The storage facility was on Martin Street across from the Highway 401 East on-ramp.

Andy was awake and making cooing sounds from the safety of his car seat as Jean carried him to the entrance.

The unit that Jock had rented was at the end of a cinderblock corridor. The key fit. The lock turned and Jean stepped into the darkened interior, climate controlled if the warm air that abruptly engulfed her was any indication. She flipped a wall switch and the overhead lights blazed to life, illuminating a plain cherrywood desk and a swivel chair.

A manila envelope lay on the desktop.

Jean placed Andy on the desk and then sat in the chair and picked up the envelope. Inside was a single sheet of paper. A handwritten note read:

Jean,

By now you have found the key and are sitting in my storage room, reading this. You needn't bother looking around. There is nothing else in here but this final letter to you. And yes, if you and everyone else is still wondering, I did decide to end it, although don't ask me how, because I haven't quite decided that yet. Something dramatic for sure. Don't spend a lot of time fretting over why I've done this. The answer is simple: I've made enough mess of things, and don't choose to face any more consequences than I already have. Putting myself and you and the town through the embarrassment of a murder trial is too much. Everyone will wonder if there isn't something else, secret files that would incriminate others around me, that sort of thing.

Well, there isn't anything like that.

My sometimes-dubious association with Del Caulder is well known. I did a lot of things over the years to support Del and to line my own pockets, but it never went any further than that. The police—and you for that matter—can look around to your heart's content but there is nothing else to find.

I know I've disappointed you and I am truly sorry. Of all the people in my life, you are the one I did not want to hurt. I've certainly failed in that desire, and I don't blame you for hating me. But please, as the years pass, try your best to forgive me, and always keep in mind that no matter what happened, I loved you very much.

Jean dropped the letter back on the desk. Nearby, Andy stirred and made complaining noises. "You know, little guy," she said. "You are absolutely right.

There's something wrong here. Beginning with a something you may not have noticed."

She held the letter up in front of him. He made a half-hearted grab for it. "Do you see what I see?"

Andy made more noises.

"Okay, you don't see it, but I do."

She replaced the letter on the desk and then spent minutes going through the drawers. They all were empty.

Standing, she picked up the baby seat. Andy looked pleased to be once more on the move. Jean took a last look around the barren room, confused as to why Jock would ever have rented it in the first place.

Unless.

Unless there had been more here at one time.

Taking the letter, she replaced it in the envelope before lifting up Andy. Outside in the darkened lot, the night air had cooled. Jean could hear the distant rumble of traffic as she approached the car and opened the back door. She placed Andy in the back. Only then did she hear a sound behind her.

She had started to turn around when a blow to her head sent her staggering forward. She collapsed against the car, vaguely heard Andy loudly wailing before she was yanked back, hitting rough pavement. There was another blow and this time all the lights went out.

31

Eve had arrived home, changed into her sweats, and poured herself a glass of Merlot, attempting to put the rigors of the day out of her mind, at least for a few minutes.

Then Amy appeared, tired and drawn, and it was apparent the bad day was not over.

"I just got off the phone with the Milton police chief," Amy said in a voice drained of energy. "It's what we feared. The mayor's sister shot Peter Earp."

"Dead?"

"No, thank god. At least not so far. He's in intensive care at Milton District Hospital. Critical condition."

"What's the prognosis?"

"Not good. The chief says she shot him three times."

"Jesus Christ. What the hell's the matter with her?"

"Who knows what happened. The chief either didn't know or wasn't about to give out too many details. After she shot Peter, the young woman dropped the gun and waited on a park bench until the police arrived."

Eve swore again and then slumped into a chair, rubbing at her temples. "I've got a glass of wine in the other room," she said to Amy. "Would you please get it for me?"

By the time Amy returned with the wine, Eve had recovered somewhat. She took a couple of gulps that worked to add color to her cheeks. "You said something before."

"Yes," Amy said, trying to remember what she had said.

"About making this work for us."

"I don't think I said anything like that."

Eve wasn't listening. "Let's do this. Let's make it work for us."

"All right," Amy said, not liking the direction in which this was headed. "How do you propose we do that?"

"We need to get into Peter's house."

Amy felt herself tense. "I don't think that's a good idea, Eve."

"It's a damned good idea. Peter's fighting for his life. Can you think of a better time?"

"All I know is that if anything goes wrong, this comes back to bite us."

"It won't go wrong," Eve said decisively. "You have a key to his house, don't you?"

"Eve, I'm not going around to his house."

"Then get hold of Pierre Dorval. He will know what to do."

"He's an ex-Mountie, will he do this?"

"Pierre will do what's necessary," Eve replied.

"I don't like the idea of involving him," Amy said. "We're just adding another body who can give us problems down the road."

Eve gave her assistant a sharp look. Do you want to do it?"

Amy didn't say anything.

"Get hold of Pierre," Eve said.

———

Rough asphalt pressed against the side of her face.

That was Jean's first sensation. The second was the pain in her head, growing worse as she tried to raise herself off the asphalt surface.

A ringing in her ears was superseded by the wind rushing through her head. From somewhere faraway came a child's cry. Jean got to her knees, the sound of the wind subsiding a bit, allowing the child's cry to grow louder.

Andy, she thought. *Andy*.

He was still in his car seat, struggling, not happy being ignored by his bleeding, semi-conscious caregiver. She got him out of the car, held him close and like magic he stopped crying, wiggling contentedly against her chest. Unaccountably, she started to cry, holding Andy close, her head throbbing.

Weeping with relief.

Her head cleared a little more. Blood continued to trickle down her forehead. She ignored it. Using the side of the car to brace herself, she rose to her feet, holding Andy. She searched around for the manila envelope. It wasn't on the ground where it must have fallen when she was hit.

Her attacker had taken it.

32

Hooked up to IV and morphine drips and breathing through an oxygen mask, Peter Earp appeared to be resting quietly.

The regular up and down rhythm of his chest was reassuring, Mickey Dann thought, standing near Peter's bed in the ICU at Milton District Hospital.

"He's been shot three times," the emergency room doctor was saying. "Once in the chest, again in his left arm. A third shot to the abdomen. We performed surgery to remove the bullets from his chest and abdomen. We cut open the abdominal cavity, discovered that the bullet had pierced his stomach, repaired that, and removed the bullet. The bullet in his arm shattered the ulna—that's the thinner and longer of the two forearm bones—so we've had to insert a metal plate to repair it. It was too risky to remove the bullet in his arm, so it's been left where it is."

More information than Mickey needed but the doctor was obviously proud of what had been accomplished. After all, it was not every day a critically injured gunshot victim arrived at Milton District Hospital.

"You saved his life," Mickey said.

"We got lucky. The patient was on his way here within ten minutes of being shot. Also, the shooter used a small caliber pistol. They cause less damage than, say, a rifle. But, still, there's damage to his internal organs."

"You'll keep us up to date?" Mickey said.

"Certainly," the doctor said.

In the waiting room outside the ER, Mickey found himself confronted by Amar Bal accompanied by a familiar figure—Eddie Fitzpatrick, the sleek, white-haired attorney who over the years had represented Jock Whitlock and now appeared to represent the acting mayor.

"Detective Mann, have you got a moment for Mayor Bal?" Eddie Fitzpatrick called out.

"I am the acting mayor," Amar announced insistently. He held out his hand to Mickey. "We have not met before."

Mickey took the offered hand reluctantly, saying, "I'm afraid there is not much I can tell you, sir. I really shouldn't be talking to you."

"I understand that, Detective," Eddie interjected. "However, Mr. Bal would like to make a statement in connection with this tragic, regrettable incident."

"Then we should do it properly at police headquarters," Mickey said.

"He was blackmailing me," Amar burst out angrily. "A duplicitous individual. He was blackmailing me so that I would agree to his development. He involved my sister. That is why she shot him. He pushed her beyond the brink, this dreadful, evil man."

Mickey looked at Eddie Fitzpatrick. "You know this is not the way to do this."

"Yes, but Mr. Bal feels there is important information you should have as you pursue your investigation of this tragic matter."

Mickey addressed the acting mayor. "Please, come to my office tomorrow at ten. Bring Mr. Fitzpatrick with you. I'll take your statement then." He turned to Eddie. "Is that agreeable?"

"I'll have the mayor there at ten," Eddie said.

"He is an evil man." Amar's voice broke with emotion. "There is a good reason why my sister did what she did. An excellent reason!"

Mickey walked away leaving Amar Bal trembling beside his lawyer.

———————

"Given what's happened, they're after a warrant to search Peter Earp's house so if you're going to take action, better do it fast," Pierre Dorval said to Amy Wu-Chan when they met in the morning on Queen's Park Crescent. Pierre had finished his daily run; Amy was about to begin hers.

"That's my thinking," Amy said as she passed him one of the two Starbucks coffees she had brought with her. "Any action on our part must be quick but discreet. Do you have someone in mind?"

"I've got the guy," Pierre said. He took a sip of his coffee. "It requires bringing him in from out of town and he doesn't come cheap. But he'll get the job done."

"If you vouch for this person, that's fine," Amy said. "I don't want to know much more than that."

"There is the problem of how to get into the house," Pierre said. "I prefer that it doesn't look like a break and enter. That will only make for more complications."

"That's easy," Amy said. "I can provide you with the key."

"What about an alarm system."

"No problem. I have the code that disarms it."

Pierre raised his eyebrows slightly, the single indication that Amy's statements surprised him. "And the house is empty?"

"As far as I know," Amy said.

"Then my guy can slip in and out again and no one's the wiser. Good."

"Let's move ahead," Amy declared. "But tell your people they have to be careful. Private police patrol the neighborhood. They know all the locals and are aware of strangers. Also, there are lots of CCTV cameras."

"Not to worry. These people know what they're doing. But there is one more thing," Pierre said.

"What's that?"

"They can get in the house. All that will work out. The thing is…"

"Yes?"

"Once inside, what's my guy looking for?"

33

A shallow gash along the edge of the hairline, nothing all that serious. Certainly she had experienced worse, Jean told herself, gazing into the bathroom mirror so that she could clean the wound with soap and water and then apply disinfectant.

She hated looking into a mirror. Someone pale and beaten by life—not to mention unknown assailants— always stared back; an unforgiving portrait of herself, this one done in bloodstains.

The sound of Andy drew her out of herself. She changed his diaper, fed him again, sat holding him while he gently inspected the contours of her battered face as though understanding that his caregiver had been hurt and he must be gentle. His eyes were full of merriment as he poked at her nose. A happy baby, she thought. How long was that going to last? Well, she was going to ensure it did.

Somehow.

Jean carried Andy up to her bedroom and lay down with him. He settled into the crook of her arm. That was better, she thought. Her head didn't hurt quite so much. She would lie here for a time, long enough to get her strength back.

For a moment, she would close her eyes.

Just for a moment.

Then her phone began making noises. Jean jerked awake in pitch darkness, her head swimming in pain, no idea how long she had been out. Andy stirred beside her.

"How is it that yours is one of the last numbers Peter Earp called before he was shot?" The demanding, agitated voice of Mickey Dann.

Jean was trying to clear her head. "What time is it?" she asked, reaching for the light on the bedside table.

"It's late but we're up to our ears in shit over this shooting. Practically the first name that comes up is yours. How the hell is that?"

"How is Peter? Is he all right?"

"He's still alive but critical. She shot him three times."

"She shot him? Who? Who shot him?"

"Where have you been? It's all over the news. Amar Bal's sister."

"She shot Peter?" Her throbbing head was having trouble digesting this.

"You haven't answered my question, Jean. Why was Peter Earp trying to get in touch with you?"

"If that was the case, I didn't get his call," Jean said.

"Jean…"

"Okay, okay. I'm doing some work for him."

"What kind of work?"

She took a deep breath, trying to rid herself of the buzz in her head. "I'd better talk to Peter before I say too much more," Jean said.

"Jean, don't screw around with me," Mickey said angrily. "I'm the guy standing between you and Petrusiak. If it was up to him, he'd have you in jail."

"Why would he do something like that?"

"I don't think he likes you."

"Now why in the world wouldn't he like me?"

"Part of it is because he thinks I like you."

"Is that true, Mickey? Do you like me?"

Mickey ignored the question. "The other part—the important part—he believes you're lying to us. About everything."

"Look, for what it's worth, I don't think what I've done for Peter has anything to do with his being shot."

"Amar Bal is about to give us a statement saying Peter was blackmailing his sister so that he would agree to go ahead with a fairgrounds development he's trying to push through. Needless to say, this is about to blow up into a huge scandal. If you're involved in any way or if you have information that might be useful to our investigation, I need to know."

The accusation that Peter might be involved in blackmail caught Jean by surprise. "I don't know anything about that," she said. "If anything, he was worried someone was trying to extort him."

"Fair warning, Jean, they're bringing in the OPP to investigate local corruption. They're going to want to talk to you about your association with Peter Earp. My advice is that you don't lie to them."

"You never answered my question," Jean said.

"What question?"

"The one about whether you like me."

"Good-bye, Jean."

Mickey clicked off the line.

She was struggling out of bed when her cell phone sounded again. She thought it might be Mickey calling back to tell her he was only kidding, he really did like her.

But it wasn't Mickey.

"Hey, Jean," Max Flagg said.

"Who's this?" Jean asked knowing all too well who it was.

"Who the hell do you think it is?"

"Why are you calling me, Max?"

"You wanted me to call you," Max insisted.

"I thought it was the other way around."

"I said I might have something for you."

"That's what you said, Max."

"As it happens, I may have something."

"As it happens?"

"Tonight. Eight o'clock."

"That's not much notice."

"You in or not?"

"What? You gotta rewire a house? I'm not going to be much use to you."

"The dress is business casual."

"You're kidding. There's a dress code?"

"Business casual. Be at the shop at eight."

Jean was about to tell him she had a baby to consider and wasn't sure she could meet him. But before she could say anything, he hung up.

Andy was making the sounds that signified he wanted attention. She picked him up and held him.

"What am I going to do with you, little man? I've got to go off with some bad guys and I don't think you should come along."

Andy mewed happily.

She thought about it for a time and then telephoned Grace Travis. "This is a pleasant surprise," Grace said.

"I'd like you to do me a favor, if you can," Jean said.

"What can I do to help?"

"How are your babysitting skills?"

That produced silence on the other end of the line. "Did I hear you correctly?" Grace asked.

"You did," Jean agreed.

"I shouldn't, I suppose, but I have difficulty thinking of you as a mother."

"Believe me, I'm as surprised as you are. It's only temporary."

"I see. When do you need me?"

"Tonight. At about seven."

"I can't believe I'm saying this," Grace said. "But I'll be there. And you know what, Jean? I'm not even going to ask questions. Questions like, how did you end up with a baby? I'm not going to ask that."

"You're a sweetheart," Jean said.

"No, I'm not. It's simply that I have to see this for myself."

Jean spent time after getting off the phone working on her makeup, doing the best she could to hide the gash on her forehead. Her best didn't work very well. Tough shit, she decided. Max would just have to put up with the wounded version of herself.

Once she finished with her makeup, she went to her closet looking for something to wear. Not a lot of choice. Particularly not in the business casual department.

Whatever that was.

A simple black dress would have to do. Why, she even had a shoulder bag to match the dress. When she had put everything together, she inspected herself in the mirror. Not exactly the picture of seduction, providing that's what Max was after, but the imperfection reflected back at her would have to do.

She slung the bag over her shoulder. One final accessory probably necessary when planning an evening with Max Flagg.

The Glock automatic.

34

A white Cadillac Escalade, gleaming in the failing evening light, was parked inside the chain-link fence at Fortress Dynamic Electric. At first as she approached, Jean thought no one was inside but then the front door opened. One of Max's long-haired goons appeared and motioned for her to hurry. "Get your ass in here," he said. "Max is waiting."

She tried to remember the goon's name? Burke?

"Burke, isn't it?"

"That's right," Burke said.

"Aren't you a nice guy," Jean said dryly.

"Max didn't hire either one of us because we're nice," he replied.

"Say, you're not as dumb as you look," she said.

"There's hope for me."

"No, there isn't," Jean said. "I only like guys who are as dumb as they look."

She stepped past the hot-eyed Burke into the interior.

Max was in his office looking a little more comfortable than he had previously. He scowled when he saw her.

"Jesus Christ, what happened to you?"

Obviously, the makeup hadn't worked. "I'm like you, Max, I keep running into doors."

She was aware of Burke behind her. Max stared past her at him. "You see her?" he demanded.

"She'll have to do," Burke said.

"Listen, I don't have to be here," Jean said. "I can walk out the door any time."

Max struggled to his feet. "Forget it. Too late to change plans. Let's get out of here."

"Where are we going?" Jean asked.

Max frowned. "You want to work for me? Quit asking questions. Keep your mouth shut and do as your told. You got that?"

"Sure, Max," Jean said slowly. "I got that."

"Let's get into it," Max said.

They went out to the Escalade and Burke got behind the wheel. Max told Jean to sit in the passenger seat. He would ride in the back.

As night fell, Burke drove the Escalade north on Bronte and then turned right onto Steeles to Martin Street and then, somewhat to Jean's surprise swung onto the on-ramp leading to the 401 Highway east toward Toronto.

Is that where they were headed? Jean wondered.

Traffic at this time of night was heavy although it could be argued that traffic on the 401 was increasingly unbearable day or night. Tonight, it was particularly bad, stop and go, with Burke squirming impatiently and repeating "Shit!" every few minutes.

"Jesus Christ, calm down," Max ordered from the back. "You're driving me crazy."

"Goddamn traffic," Burke snarled.

"Take it easy," Max called tensely.

"I'm fine. Jesus Christ! Get off my back."

"I'm not on your back, asshole."

Burke said something under his breath Jean didn't quite catch.

The fighting shitheads, Jean thought.

———————

Max leaned forward and put his hand on Jean's shoulder. She did not like the feel of that hand. Closer, his breath was hot on her ear. "Here's the thing. We're going into a neighborhood in Toronto, okay?"

"Okay with me, Max," Jean said,

"The Bridal Path. You know it?"

"I've heard of it," Jean acknowledged. "What? You're thinking of buying a house?"

"Yeah, you might say that. I've got my eye on a place. We're going to take a look at it."

"At this time of night?"

"Why not?" said Max. "Here's where you come in, Jean. Burke and me, we start wandering around that neighborhood, we attract attention we don't want. But you, a good-looking, well-dressed woman being dropped off at the house where she's staying, no one takes any notice."

"What am I supposed to do once you drop me off?"

"You go inside, for Christ's sake, what do you think you do?"

"All right, take it easy," Jean said. "You want to tell me how I get inside? Or do I break the door down?"

"Try using this, instead." He handed her a key. "That'll get you in the front door."

"What about an alarm system?"

"I'm going to give you the code."

"All right, I'm inside. Then what?"

"I'll let you know when we get there."

Max sat back, lost in the dimness, ending the conversation.

Jean gazed down at the house key in her hand. She thought, What the hell have I gotten myself into?

35

Burke finally turned the Escalade off the 401 south on Bayview where the traffic remained heavy but kept moving. He slowed to make a left turn onto the Bridal Path and abruptly the world was peaceful and quiet, the wide, leafy street before them deserted, the traffic sounds a muted distraction far, far away.

In the land of the rich, Jean concluded, there were no loud noises, only comfortable—and comforting—silence. Light occasionally peeked out through thick foliage on either side of the road, suggesting that Toronto's elite occupied their gargantuan houses and were not receiving visitors this evening. Certainly not an Escalade containing a couple of Milton hoods who were, to say the least, way out of their element.

"Jesus H. Christ," breathed Burke as he crept slowly along the street. "Who the hell lives here?"

"A bunch of pricks," Max announced.

"Where do I sign up to join the pricks?" asked Burke.

"Ahead on the right," Max said quietly. "Number thirty-three. Should be an open drive. Pull up just before it."

Burke did as he was ordered. Max's hot breath was back on Jean's ear. His voice had become tense. "What we're gonna do, we gonna drive up to the front of the house and let you off. You use the key to unlock the door and go inside. The alarm key pad is to the right of the door."

"Okay," Jean said. "But then what?"

"Then you find what I want you to find."

"What?"

"A flash drive. There's an office. It's probably in there."

"*Probably?* What do you mean *probably?*"

"An office. That's all I know."

"It's not much," Jean said.

"Make it happen," Max snapped. He handed her a flip phone. "When you're finished, open this up. We'll come and get you."

"Okay," Jean said.

She grabbed her purse from where she had placed it on the floor. Burke stopped her. "You don't need that."

Jean thought of the gun. She turned so that he could see her reassuring smile. "A woman gets out of a car without a purse? Not likely, providing you want to play this out the way it should be played out."

He thought about this for an instant. "Okay, take it." He patted Burke on the shoulder. "Let's do it."

A flagstone drive circled the hazy outline of a big two-story Georgian house. The home of an English country gentleman. At least one could pretend to be an English country gentleman. The house would give you a good start at the disguise.

As the Escalade drove away, Jean inserted the key into the front door lock. A smooth click of the lock's tumblers and she opened the door and stepped inside. Even in the dark, the house breathed the luxury provided by an expensive interior designer who could offer everything except a sense that anyone lived here.

Jean found the alarm panel, keyed in the code. It worked. The system announced that it was disarmed. She breathed out and then moved through a series of tastefully decorated rooms until she found an office.

Big windows interrupted floor-to-ceiling bookshelves. She flipped a light switch and the room was abruptly suffused with light, illuminating a desk the size of a pool table with nothing on it but a laptop. Framed photographs were displayed on a trestle table pushed against a wall near the desk. Peter Earp with Canada's prime minister. Peter in a hard hat with a group of dignitaries, a construction site in the background. Peter with Ontario premier Eve Harriot. Amy Wu-Chan smiled beside them.

Shit.

Here she was creeping around Peter Earp's darkened Bridal Path mansion in search of a flash drive for Milton's number one bad guy who somehow had a key to the place.

It didn't seem believable on any number of levels. And yet here she was.

Jean moved from the trestle table to the desk. A silver flash drive protruded from the side of the laptop. Is this what she was supposed to be looking for? It seemed too easy. She turned on the laptop, waited until it flared to life and then tried to get in, almost immediately discovering what she thought she would discover—Peter's computer life was password-protected.

She removed the flash drive and dropped it into her shoulder bag and then went through the desk looking for other flash drives. There were none, at least none that she could find. She was closing the bottom drawer when she heard the noise. She paused, not moving.

Listening.

The sound of a door closing.

36

Someone else was in the house.

Jean slipped over to the light switch and turned off the light. In darkness she stood still, listening to the sound of footsteps coming toward the office. She pressed herself against the wall.

The office door opened slowly. A foot appeared, paused, and then the huge bulk of Max Flagg materialized out of the dark.

"Max," she said, stepping away from the wall to confront him. "What the hell are you doing here?"

"Did you find it?" he demanded. In shadow, he was an almost feral presence, a threatening aura.

She hesitated and then said, "No, I didn't find anything."

"Shit. It's got to be here."

"You sure it's in this office?"

"That's what they told me."

They? Jean thought. Out loud, she said, "Do you have any idea whose house this is?"

"What difference does that make?"

"Take a look at the photographs on the table over there."

Max went over and peered down at the photos. "Holy shit," he breathed. "It's goddamn Peter Earp."

"He's the developer, isn't he?"

Max straightened and turned to her. "You know him?"

"I've seen him on television. Someone shot him, right?"

Max shook his head and laughed. "Man, this is incredible," he said gleefully. "I've got more shit on this guy back at the office. Now this."

"Yeah? Max the blackmailer, is that it?"

"Max the guy who protects his ass," he amended.

"Impressive," Jean said. "What have you got on him?"

The merry look of triumph disappeared, replaced by a more typical expression of suspicion. "Why would you give a shit?"

"Are you serious? We've just broken into his house. What are we doing here if you've got something on him? Maybe you don't have anything. How should I know?"

He loomed close to her. "Don't mess with me."

"I'm not messing with you, Max."

"That's good," he said. His closeness made Jean uncomfortable. "You like to push buttons, don't you?"

"Not me," Jean said.

Before she could stop him, he mashed his mouth against hers.

She yanked away. "What are you doing?"

"Maybe looking for a little bit of what you've got on offer," he said, advancing. "I mean, even banged up a bit, you look pretty damned good."

"Nothing is on offer, Max. Let's get out of here."

"Maybe I can change your mind," he said. He tried to kiss her again. She ducked away.

He slapped her hard across the face and that sent her reeling back. He was on her, tearing at her dress.

She fell to the floor with him groping on top of her. The weight of him was like a refrigerator had fallen on her. She could hardly move or breathe. Her out-stretched hand touched something. Her shoulder bag must have fallen to the floor when he hit her. She man-aged to turn her head. She could just make out the bag in the dimness. The flap was open. Her fingers fumbled to reach inside. Meanwhile, Max was fighting against her writhing legs to lift her skirt.

Her straining fingers touched the bag's flap, curled around it, pulling the bag towards her. Meantime, he rose up so that he could unbuckle his belt. That gave her the moment she needed to pull the Glock from inside the bag. As he came down on her again, she slammed the Glock against the side of his head.

Max grunted, seemingly more stunned than hurt. But the blow stopped him, and that gave her the open-ing she needed to hit him again. This time he sagged off her. She scrambled to her feet, leaving him on the floor, holding his head.

Jean stood over him, pointing the Glock, uncertain what he was going to do. He did nothing except lie still, bleeding on Peter Earp's expensive sisal carpet. She backed out of the room and then made her way back through the house.

At the front door, she paused remembering that Burke was somewhere outside. She readied the Glock, took a deep breath and stepped into the cool night air.

The Escalade was parked in the drive, the motor running, Burke lounging against it smoking a cigarette. He looked up startled, as she strode toward him.

"Where's Max?" he asked.

Jean pointed the gun at him. "Move away from the vehicle," she ordered in her best tough-Mountie voice, the voice she could adopt for confronting lowlifes like Burke.

"What the hell," he said, but did not move.

"Burke, I'm not going to tell you again, move away from the vehicle."

"Godamn bitch," he said, but he complied, sliding a few feet away, his body tensed like a gunslinger ready to go for his gun.

Keeping the Glock trained on him, Jean moved to the driver's-side door and opened it. Slipping inside, she closed the door. Through the windshield, she could see Burke lunge forward, the cigarette dangling incongruously from the corner of his mouth.

She shoved the Escalade into drive and hit the gas hard. The vehicle clipped Burke, sending him flying backward.

Jean spun the Escalade around and with a screech of tires shot down the drive onto the street.

Reaching Bayview, she took her foot off the gas, slowing the Escalade, joining the thin line of cars on the street at this time of night.

Easing her grip on the wheel.

Calming.

37

Jean parked the Escalade beside her car at Dynamic Electric.

A metal ring full of keys was in one of the cupholders on the console. From inside the cinderblock structure, she could hear the relentless bark of the German Shepherd. Not so much a bark, Jean thought when she got out of the Escalade, more a hurting cry.

An animal in pain.

It took her several tries before she got the key that opened the front door. Inside, she kept the lights off, rounding the counter to the closed office door. She could hear the dog's cries from the other side. Tentatively, she turned the knob and opened the door a crack, expecting the dog to jump up at her. But there was only the sound of pained cries falling to whimpers.

She opened the door wider and stepped into Max's cluttered mess of an office. Otis lay on the floor in front of Max's desk. When he saw Jean in the doorway, he raised his head slightly, baring his jaws in a warning snarl.

But not for long. He didn't have the energy to sustain the snarl. Panting, he returned his head to the floor.

Jean stepped around the dog to the desk.

"I've got more shit on this guy back at the office."

"Okay, Max," Jean said out loud. "Where did you hide the shit?" She opened the top drawer. Piles of yellowish invoices, a check book that didn't look as though Max had used it much, business cards from various vendors and beneath it all, a manila file folder.

Jean pulled the file out and laid it on the desk. Inside were six eight-by-ten photographs that looked as if they had been taken from a big television screen. The dimly lit bedroom muted the color but there was no doubt, Peter Earp was on a bed with Eve Harriot, the premier of Ontario. Three of the photographs featured Amy Wu-Chan entwined with Eve and Peter. None of the subjects in the photos had any clothes on.

She closed the file, distracted by renewed whimpers from Otis.

Tentatively, she kneeled to the dog. His chest heaved, but this time he did not snarl. Blood was matted into his thick coat. More blood caked around his ears. Otis raised his head slightly when she ran a gentle hand along his body as though desperate for any kind of human contact. And was that a beseeching look she saw in his eyes? No, couldn't be, she thought. Dogs couldn't give you beseeching looks.

Could they?

She rose to her feet, forced herself to move away. "There's nothing I can do for you, fella," she said to him. "I'm afraid you're on your own."

In response, Otis lowered his head, issuing a long, low whimper as if deeply disappointed by Jean's words. She closed her eyes. She wasn't seeing this. What could she do? She was helpless.

Taking the file folder from the desk, she headed out of the office. She got as far as the door before she stopped. She wasn't going to look back at the dog whimpering on the floor. If she did that, she was lost.

She turned and looked at him.

Shit. Damn. Hell!

She went back to where the dog lay. He raised his head. "Don't look at me like that," she said to him. "You're only going to get the two of us in trouble."

She saw a leash hanging on the wall, removed it, and leaned down to attach it to the dog's collar. Then she tucked her hands slowly beneath his thin, supple body so she could lift him up. She thought for sure he would object and rally what strength he had left to attack. But it was as if the dog sensed she was there to help, not to hurt. He lay limply in her arms as she staggered under the weight of him and struggled to her feet.

Jean carried Otis through the office and out the door. In the parking lot, his heaviness forced her to put him down. She was on her knees panting, debating how she was ever going to get him into the car. Abruptly, he rose onto his haunches, cocking his head as if wondering what she was up to.

She got to her feet and he allowed her to lead him to the car. She opened the rear door, thinking about how she could get him into the back. Otis solved the problem by putting his paws up on the seat. She lifted him by the hind quarters. He yelped as she slid him along the seat, then he stretched out and lay quietly.

Once she was satisfied that Otis was settled, Jean hurried back into the office, collected the file, locked the front door and returned to her car.

As she got behind the wheel, she saw that Otis was sitting up. Was she seeing things, or did the dog look happy?

No, she thought as she drove onto the street, dogs couldn't look happy. Not vicious dogs like Otis who could rip your throat out with one snap of his jaws.

Could he?

38

Grace was reading a book on the sofa beside a sleeping Andy when Jean came in with Otis on his leash. Grace's eyes widened when she saw the two of them.

"Don't ask," Jean said.

Grace responded with one of her gentle smiles. "A baby and now a dog," she observed. "You're becoming domesticated, Jean."

"I'm going crazy," Jean countered. "How's Andy been?"

"He's a dream," Grace pronounced. "All that little guy seems to need is a hug and he's as happy as can be."

All any of us need, Jean mused. But hugs were in short supply these days.

Otis, meanwhile, had stretched out on the floor, his breathing no longer labored. Jean went into the kitchen found a cereal bowl and filled it with water. As soon as she put it down, Otis was up, padding into the kitchen, slurping at the water. He finished it in seconds. Jean got him some more and he went at that as well.

Jean found a larger metal bowl from under the counter, filled it with the kibble she had bought at the Superstore on the way home and then added some of the pre-cooked chicken she had also purchased.

Otis hoovered it down while Jean and Grace watched. "What are you going to do with him?" asked Grace.

"I have no idea," Jean answered. "Would you like something to drink? I do believe I need a glass of wine."

"A tiny glass for me," Grace said. As she spoke, she held her thumb and forefinger a fraction apart.

They sat with their wine in the living room, Andy sleeping, Otis lying on the blanket Jean had found for him. Jean said, "I went through the bank boxes you gave me."

"What did you do with them?" Grace asked. "I don't see them anywhere."

"That's because someone broke in here and stole them."

"You're not serious," Grace said in a surprised voice.

"Not once, but twice."

"That's so ridiculous," Grace said. "There's nothing in those boxes worth stealing."

"That's what I thought, too. Someone obviously wasn't convinced. However, they didn't get the key to Jock's storage unit."

"No?"

"Thanks to you, I had the address and went around there. The unit was empty except for a letter."

"There was a letter?" Jean got the impression Grace was attempting to sound even more surprised. Not with a great deal of success, she thought.

"From Jock. Addressed to me. Did you know about it?"

"No, how could I know about it?"

"The letter amounts to a suicide note. Jock explains that he decided to take his life because he had provided everyone around him with enough pain. He didn't want to face the trauma of a murder trial."

"That sounds like Jock," Grace offered.

Jean shook her head. "No it doesn't, Grace. That's the thing. It doesn't sound like Jock at all. It sounds like you."

"Me? How could it possibly sound like me?"

"Probably because you wrote the letter. I mean, you did a pretty good job of forging his handwriting. Except it wasn't his. Not his words. Not his writing."

Grace's whole body had tensed. "This is totally ridiculous. Why would I write that letter?"

"I'm not sure, Grace. Maybe you can tell me. Also, I don't believe Jock had that unit just so he could leave me a suicide note. What else was in there and what did you do with it?"

Grace stood abruptly. Otis lifted his head and looked at her expectantly. "It's time for me to leave."

"Look, Grace. I know you're trying to do the right thing by Jock but covering for him isn't the way to do it."

"I'm not doing that," Grace said tightly.

"Then what are you doing?"

"Good night, Jean. Thank you for the wine."

Jean stood, causing Otis to rise up, wagging his tail. "Thanks for looking after Andy," she said.

"I'd be happy to do it again," Grace said, forcing a wan smile. "Perhaps without the insinuating questions next time."

"I'll do my best," Jean said.

"I'm sure you will," Grace said icily.

She marched out of the house.

Jean looked down at Otis, still wagging his tail. "I think I pissed her off. I believe I piss everyone off. What about you, Otis? Are you pissed at me, too?"

Otis continued to wag his tail.

"I need to clean you up a bit, pal," Jean said.

He wagged his tail some more and then followed her into the kitchen. Jean got a facecloth and then went at him with soap and water. He yelped a bit as she touched at various bruises along his chest and hindquarters, but otherwise stoically endured her ministrations. "Poor fella, they haven't treated you well, have they?" Jean spoke to him as she used a big towel to gently dry the areas she had washed.

When she finished, he padded away into the other room. Jean cleaned up and then poured another glass of wine. She carried it into the living room to check on Otis. He lay on the sofa, nestled beside Andy. Dog and baby together. Andy gurgled. Otis panted. Jean couldn't quite believe what she was seeing. What had become of her? Had she been transformed into the benevolent mistress of the Happy Valley Home for Neglected Children and Abused Dogs? There they were, the cooing baby and the nuzzling dog. Who would ever have guessed?

Jean took her wine into the den where she had her laptop. Otis hopped off the sofa and followed, crouched on his haunches beside her while she inserted the flash drive from Peter's house into the USB port.

"What do you think, Otis?" she said aloud. "What is it your master wanted so badly?"

The flash drive contained a Real Player video clip. She clicked on it and almost immediately the view from a distance of a dimly lit bedroom dominated by a king-size bed filled her computer screen.

Minutes passed, Jean beginning to think there would be nothing but the camera view of the bedroom, before a figure entered. Initially, given the low lighting, Jean couldn't tell who the figure was. When she finally recognized the person, she couldn't help but smile.

Soon a second figure joined the first person. And then a third appeared.

The live action version of the photographs she had found in Max's office.

Now Jean understood what all the fuss was about.

39

The video played for five minutes and twenty seconds.

When Jean had finished watching, she shut down her laptop and withdrew the flash drive. She collected the Glock from her purse and grabbed the retractable police baton which she kept against the backsplash in the kitchen. She picked up the handbag containing the file from Dynamic Electric and the flash drive and climbed the stairs to her bedroom.

Otis padded up eagerly behind her. "Don't get any ideas about sleeping with me," she said to the dog." He just gave her a look.

Downstairs again, she collected the sleeping Andy, checked to ensure he didn't require a diaper change—he didn't, thank goodness—turned off the lights and then carried him up to her bedroom.

As she entered, Otis raised his head, welcoming her to what he apparently considered his bed, seeing as how he had already staked out his place at the bottom. "I told you, you can't sleep on the bed," Jean announced to the room. "*My* bed," she added.

Otis merely cocked his head.

She deposited Andy at the head of the bed away from Otis, who promptly turned to inspect this new arrival. Andy's presence didn't appear to make a whole lot of difference to him. Jean issued a resigned sigh and then undressed and got into her pajamas. Images from the video flashed through her mind as she washed her hands and face, struck suddenly by the enormity of the difficulty in which she now found herself. She knew far too much about things she wasn't supposed to know anything about.

A man was dead. People were being blackmailed. She had been out housebreaking, beating up the town's worst badass criminal—twice—and then running over his henchman and stealing his dog.

And let's not forget the missing woman's baby sleeping in her bed. What on earth was she thinking? Or was she thinking at all?

"Not thinking, that's for damned sure," she concluded aloud, crawling under the covers, careful not to disturb the baby.

Otis lifted his large head as though curious whether she was addressing him. "But I'm not talking to you, Otis, okay?" she said to him. "I can't be sitting here in the middle of the night with a baby that isn't mine talking to a dog I've stolen. All this is crazy enough without talking to you about it. I hope you understand that."

Otis pricked up his ears.

Jean turned on her side beneath the covers. If she was rational like other people, if she led any kind of life that could be categorized as normal, she would not be in this trouble in the first place. But she wasn't rational and her life was nowhere near normal.

She rolled over to inspect Andy. Couldn't help smiling. Not a normal life at all.

Except for the baby beside her and the big dog at the end of the bed.

"That's pretty close to normal, don't you think, Otis?" But Otis already had fallen into a deep sleep, his torso raising up and down rhythmically.

Normal. Or what passed for it.

And kind of nice.

————————

The next morning, Jean got Andy fed, his diaper changed, and poured kibble into a bowl for Otis. He devoured his breakfast while Jean sipped coffee and tried to decide what to do next. The telephone rang. A ringing telephone these days was never a good thing.

Sure enough.

"It's me," Mickey Dann said when she swiped her phone open.

"Are we at the point where you only have to say, 'it's me' and I know who it is?" Jean asked.

"Apparently," Mickey said.

"You're calling to ask me for a date."

"You keep asking me that. I'm beginning to think you're serious."

"I'm hoping you'll ask me out so I can tell you I'm not going out with you."

"In that case, I'm glad I'm not asking you out."

"Then why do you keep calling?"

"Because you keep getting yourself into shit," Mickey said.

"What have I done now?"

"I've just been on the phone with the Metro Toronto police."

"Your old pals," Jean said.

"Early this morning, they arrested Max Flagg and Burke Murdoch."

"Who is Burke Murdoch?" As if she didn't know.

"One of the dickheads who works for Max."

"That's a good thing, isn't it? Keep bad guys off the streets."

"They found Max inside Peter Earp's house on the Bridal Path in Toronto. Burke was outside, lying on the pavement, his leg broken. Someone had driven off with their Cadillac Escalade."

"What were they doing at Peter Earp's house?"

"Good question. I was hoping you might have the answer."

"Why would I have any idea what they were doing?"

"We found their Escalade parked in the lot at Dynamic Electric this morning. Whoever beat up Max and then ran over his partner, drove their car back to Milton."

"And that is important because?"

"Tell me where you were last night."

"I was at home taking care of a baby," Jean promptly answered.

Mickey sighed and said, "Someone can verify that for us, can they?"

"Grace Travis dropped by for a glass of wine. How's that for an alibi?"

"When was this?"

"About eight o'clock."

"How long did she stay?"

"About three hours. She left at eleven o'clock."

"And she can confirm this?"

"Why wouldn't she?"

"Because you're lying to me? How's that for a reason?"

"You keep accusing me of lying when I'm not lying," she said.

"There you go, you're lying about not lying."

"I'm hanging up," she said.

"Don't hang up," Mickey said.

She hung up.

"Bastard," she said to her cell phone. She looked down at Otis who was gazing up at her, that expectant look on his face again. "All men are bastards," she said to him. He cocked his head. "Except you," she added.

40

The arraignment of Tamara Bal, charged with attempted murder, took place at the Provincial Offences Court in Milton.

As Mickey Dann expected, she pleaded not guilty and was granted bail and released in the custody of her brother, Amar, the acting mayor of Milton. Although it was speculated Amar would resign his council seat and give up the office of mayor, it had not happened yet.

Mickey followed Amar and his sister, both looking distraught, watched them navigate a throng of reporters and cameramen as they made their way to a waiting SUV and then speeded off along Steeles Avenue. Immediately, the energy drained out of the reporters, the objects of their enthusiasm having made their escape. They quickly began to fade away.

Mickey thought of Peter Earp and the frustrations of trying to interview him. He had regained consciousness and was out of intensive care. His lawyers insisted that he was still too ill to speak to police. Additionally, the Ontario Provincial Police were investigating allegations of corruption in connection with Peter's attempts to gain approval for a townhouse project at the Milton Fairgrounds. The various regional police agencies were piling on. Mickey feared he would get lost in the crowd.

He considered reporting next door to headquarters and then thought better of it. The thought of facing Glen Petrusiak and his incessant yammering about Jean Whitlock made him groan inwardly. In Toronto, Max Flagg wasn't talking but, according to detectives in the city, his sidekick Burke Murdoch was spilling what beans he could from his hospital bed.

According to Burke, a woman whose name he didn't know had accompanied him and Max to the Bridal Path house. She had entered the residence using a key Max provided. They drove away but the next thing Max ordered him back to the house. Max told Burke to wait in the Escalade while he went inside. The next thing Burke knew, the woman came out with a gun and forced Burke out of the vehicle. She then got behind the wheel and ran him over as she drove away.

When the Toronto detectives had asked Burke what the trio was doing there in the first place, Burke claimed to have no idea. Nor did he know how Max would have gotten hold of a key to the residence.

Petrusiak, for whatever reason, believed the mystery woman involved in the break-in was Jean. After all, they had seen her exit Dynamic Electric with no good explanation for why she had been there. As far as Petrusiak was concerned, there were several issues Jean was lying about beginning with the death of her uncle, Jock Whitlock. Mickey's partner was convinced that somehow everything that had gone down lately was connected and Jean was part of that connective tissue.

He wanted Jean arrested on suspicion of being involved in the Toronto burglary so that they could grill her hard and sweat the truth out of her. He believed Mickey's feelings for Jean were getting in the way of doing this. Although Petrusiak increasingly grated on him, Mickey had to wonder if his partner wasn't right. But then what exactly were his feelings for Jean? Half the time, he wanted to kill her; the other half he wanted her in bed. He smiled as he drove out of the parking lot.

Depending on the time of day, it could go either way.

The sound of Mickey's phone attached to the car's blue tooth device filled the interior. Speak of the devil, Mickey thought as he saw the caller ID on the LCD screen. "Glen, what's up?" he said as he drove along.

"You won't believe it," Petrusiak said.

"Try me," Mickey said.

"Doc Prescott has finally announced a date for a coroner's inquest."

"About time," Mickey said. "When is it?"

"Three weeks from now, on the twenty-third."

———————

Premier Eve Harriot was speaking to the Ontario Association of Fire Chiefs in the main ballroom at the Royal York Hotel. The fire chiefs had been out late the night before at Barbarian's Steak House and most of them were hungover. They had faint interest in Eve's call for increased support of volunteer fire departments across the province.

Amy Wu-Chan could almost feel Eve's words landing with monotonous thuds. Stationed to one side of the podium where the premier stood, she cringed silently, counting the minutes until this horror ended. She spotted Pierre Dorval, the premier's motherfucking, good-for-nothing head of security. Amid a scattering of desultory applause, she moved to where he had stationed himself at the back of the room.

"I remember when this was the Imperial Room," Pierre said. "It was Toronto's premiere entertainment showcase. Everyone played here. The greats. Tony Bennett. Marlene Dietrich. Guy Lombardo."

"Guy who?" Amy demanded, practically shouting the question. Nearby, several well-upholstered chiefs gave her a look.

"Guy Lombardo and his Royal Canadians," Pierre said. "They were fixtures on New Year's Eve for many years. They played regularly at the Imperial Room. Tremendous entertainment."

Pierre shifted uneasily beside her. "I understand you're upset," he said, keeping his eyes focused on the premier. "I don't blame you. I thought I could count on those people. They disappointed me."

"*Disappointed* you?" Amy had to gulp the words to hold back more shouting. "Christ, Pierre, do you have any idea how much shit we're in?"

"Max is a standup guy." Pierre kept his voice low and calm. "He's being bailed out this afternoon. So is his associate. He's a professional. He knows his best chance of getting out of this is keeping his mouth shut. I will now step in and handle this personally."

"And do what?"

"I'll do what's necessary to keep the premier and yourself out of this."

"That's not a plan, Pierre."

"At this point, the less you know about what has to be done the better for all of us."

"No more witless thugs like the two idiots you used."

"As I told you, Amy, I will handle this."

At the podium, the premier finished her speech. The fire chiefs could barely rally a round of applause.

Shit, Amy thought. I am surrounded by assholes. And two of them aren't even fire chiefs.

41

Jean had fallen into a routine with an ease that amazed her.

It was a routine she would have said was totally alien to her, the last thing she would even have imagined, let alone—there was no other word for it—*enjoyed*.

Andy would awaken around six thirty. She would get him fed, changed, and dressed. Then it was Otis's turn for his morning kibble. He looked healthier with each passing day, the various swellings administered by the nasty Max Flagg were subsiding; his coat had taken on a sheen. What's more, nothing seemed to make him happier than to be with Jean. The baby, too, fascinated him and Jean became convinced that rather than a vicious guard dog, Otis was a gentle loving soul.

As Otis chomped down his breakfast, Jean would throw on sweats and then put the baby in the stroller she had impulsively bought, convincing herself that since she had no idea how long she would have to care for Andy—dismissing thoughts that the Andy alert might go on forever—the stroller was a necessary investment.

With Otis on a lead and Andy in his stroller, it was time for their morning walk on the tree-lined streets of Old Milton. Early in the day, with the sun breaking through drifting clouds, only the dog walkers were out and the occasional mother with her babies. There were no uncomfortable questions about how a former RCMP officer too much in the news had overnight ended up with a baby and a dog.

During these walks, it was easy to forget there was a world of trouble awaiting her outside the small, loving bubble within which she had cloistered herself.

But trouble, as Jean soon discovered, was not far away.

"Hey, that dog," called out a hatchet-faced young man behind the wheel of a slowing Ford pickup truck as Jean came along Commercial Street with Otis and the baby.

"I'm sorry?" Jean cocked her head in the young man's direction, but kept moving.

"Dog looks familiar," the man in the truck said.

"Don't think so," Jean said.

"Can't remember his name. Big, vicious watch dog, wasn't he?"

"Not this guy," Jean said. "This guy's a baby." Jean continued walking.

Otis pricked up his ears, nostrils flaring, the muscles in his shoulders stiffening, sensing something he didn't like in that pickup.

Jean, praying the jerk behind the wheel would move on.

"Doesn't look like no baby to me."

Even at this distance, Jean could see the young man's face suddenly light with recognition. "Say, aren't you that Mountie?"

"Sorry?"

"The one who's been in all the papers."

"Don't know what you're talking about."

"You're not the Mountie?"

Jean remained silent, kept walking.

"Sure look like her."

The young man in the truck cast a final suspicious look in Jean's direction and then sped off.

Jean let her breath out slowly. Otis, relaxed, tail wagging, proceeding along the street, apparently happy to return to the business of walking Jean.

She allowed Otis to lead the way for a few more minutes and then guided him back toward the house, reminded, as though she should need reminding, that for all its growth and change, Milton remained essentially a small town—a small town in which everyone still tended to know everyone else. And their dogs.

And her, for that matter. The price you paid for too much exposure on local television news. She could not go parading around the streets for long and not expect to be recognized. She had to do something.

But what?

The answer eluded her on the walk back. The answer dropped away completely when she saw who was waiting for her on the porch.

"I want my baby," Blair Lalonde said.

42

Not knowing what to expect and somewhat nervous about it, Pierre Dorval waited in the designated coffee shop not far from the Juravinski Cancer Hospital in Hamilton. Pierre had ordered a latte, wondering if he had the right place since his friend, who was never late, was late.

But as the waitress set down his latte in a big white bowl, John Pesce, known to everyone around Hamilton as Johnny Fish, made his entrance.

As always, Pierre mused, you did not miss John. Tall and handsome, perfectly groomed hair the color of fine silver, dressed impeccably in a dark Hugo Boss suit, set off by a snow-white dress shirt and a perfectly knotted Hermes tie. Too bad they called him Johnny Fish—not to his face, mind you—since John Pesce looked anything but a guy named Johnny Fish.

Pierre stood and the two men greeted each other warmly, old comrades from opposite sides of a fence Pierre during his law enforcement career had slipped over more than once. Enough to get to know John and to remind himself that despite his friend's seeming warmth and openness, he remained someone you treaded around carefully.

The waitress approached, brightening as John settled into a chair. "Mister Johnny," she said. "Pleasure to see you."

"Good morning, Greta."

"Usual black coffee, Mister Johnny?"

"You always remember, Greta."

"Hey, you're Mr. Johnny."

As Greta went away, John gave Pierre one of the broad smiles he could produce when relaxed and among friends. "It's been a while," he said.

"Too long," Pierre replied.

"You're looking good, Pierre."

"And you, John. Unchanging. It's amazing."

"You're too kind," John said, "but then I can't resist a compliment. How's your health?"

"A little prostate difficulty a couple of years ago, but the doctors say they have it under control."

John nodded toward the window and the cancer hospital beyond. "I am a regular over there—and here. The coffee's very good."

"Sorry to hear that," Pierre said. "But they got it all right, didn't they?"

"Let's say the doctors are optimistic," John said. He sipped his coffee.

"They keep telling me you die with it not because of it," Pierre said.

"Let's hope they're right," John said. He put down his coffee cup. "But you didn't come here to talk to me about cancer, Pierre. What can I do for you?"

"I think maybe it's what we can do for each other," Pierre said.

"I'm always happy to hear about something that benefits me."

Pierre leaned forward and lowered his voice. "The other night two goons were arrested inside Peter Earp's house on the Bridal Path in Toronto."

"My former son-in-law. I hadn't heard."

"These bastards really screwed up. I'm having to deal with the fallout from that screw-up."

"I'm not sure I understand this, Pierre. How would a couple of stupid burglars on the Bridal Path impact you?"

"I'm sorry to say these two were under contract to me."

"To break into my son-in-law's house?"

"A job for a client," Pierre amended. "They were looking for something."

"What were they looking for?"

"I'm told it was a flash drive."

"And what was on that flash drive, Pierre?"

"I don't have that information," Pierre answered.

"I see. And did they find this whatever-you-call-it?"

"I don't believe so. The point is, whatever is on the drive was being used to extort my client."

"Peter was doing this?"

"Not in so many words but the possibility certainly was there," Pierre said.

"The possibility," John repeated softly. He appeared to take this in, finishing his coffee. "Since you work for the premier of this province, I imagine your client is the Red Queen. I am inclined to believe that she deserves what she gets. However, my son-in-law, or former son-in-law, has become an embarrassment to me and to my daughter. As you know, he's been shot by the sister of Milton's acting mayor. He's being accused of attempting to bribe the mayor and other city officials. It's a terrible mess. And now this."

"I'm sorry to add to your difficulties here, John, but I thought you should know."

"You *thought* I should know or you *think* I should do something about it?"

"I need your help," Pierre said.

"Yes, I suppose you do."

"In the short term these two men, have to be bailed out. For obvious reasons, I can't be seen doing it."

"I will contact a lawyer who is discreet and will act for you at arm's length," John said.

"Thank you, John. That would be much appreciated. However, I am concerned that in the long term these two men pose a threat. I wish I could say I could count on their silence but I'm afraid I can't."

"Who are the two involved?"

"Max Flagg. His associate is a fellow named Burke Murdoch."

John made a face. It occurred to Pierre that when he looked like that it was easy to believe he was Johnny Fish.

"Max, I know. A bastard. A dangerous, unpredictable bastard. I've tried to ignore his actions but it's not a good situation; a situation that gets the attention of local police as well as the OPP. Problems we don't need in this area."

"Like I say, they are not reliable, particularly if they find themselves staring at long prison sentences, which could well be the case."

John pushed his coffee cup to one side so that he could lean into Pierre. Johnny Fish was back. "What would you like me to do, Pierre? You have to tell me what you want."

"You are in a position that I am not," Pierre said uneasily. "You can make this problem go away. My client is spared any future embarrassment and so is your son-in-law. What is it they say? A win-win for everyone concerned."

"This is not the way I like to do business these days," John said. "These days, I like the word 'legitimate.' That's why I maintained an association with Peter after my daughter divorced him. I thought he could be a help." He shook his head sadly and then gave a wan smile. "Instead, he turns out to be a worse criminal than me, which is fine, except he is a particularly untalented criminal and that's not what I need."

"I'm sorry to put this on you, John," Pierre said. "At our ages we don't need this crap. I was hoping to be retired to my place in Florida later this year. Now, I don't think that's going to be possible."

"I'm afraid I've got more business across the street." John sat back in his chair. 'Not a happy time, I'm afraid."

The café began to fill, mostly young people who made Pierre feel suddenly old and out of place. John Pesce seemed not to notice. He glanced at his watch. "I have to go across the street in a couple of minutes to see people and listen to more news I'm probably not going to like," he said. "But let me see if I can help you. Eyes are on me thanks to my stupid son-in-law so I must be careful."

"We both must be careful," Pierre agreed.

As the noise level of the luncheon crowd began to rise, John eyed his friend balefully and asked, "Why do you do this, Pierre? I understand why I do it; this is my life. But it isn't yours. Why do you continue to get your hands dirty for these people?"

Pierre said something that got lost in the surrounding din. John leaned forward and said, "What?"

Pierre looked infinitely sad as he said, "I wish I knew."

43

Blair held baby Andy while declining to say anything about where she had been. Just hiding, that's all. But she missed her baby so much and so had to return no matter the risk.

Andy lay happily in his mother's arms. Too happily, Jean thought as she prepared a bowl of tomato soup for Blair. Jean tried not to think that she hoped it might be otherwise.

Instead, she took Andy so that Blair could go to work devouring the soup and half the baguette Jean had purchased earlier that day. Wherever she had hidden, they had not fed her properly. Also, she was in need of a shower and some clean clothes.

As Blair ate, Otis padded into view cocking his head at the stranger in his house. When Blair had first entered, Otis had bared his teeth at her. Jean could see that despite what she perceived as his gentleness, he could transform quickly into the guard dog Max had designed him to be.

As soon as Jean had ordered him to stop, the bared teeth disappeared and Otis became docile, slinking over to Jean, seeking approval. He had soon lost interest and drifted off to the other room in search of a comfortable sofa.

Now he was back sniffing in Blair's direction, not hostile, just curious.

"I don't like dogs," Blair said.

"Otis is friendly," Jean reassured. "Andy loves him."

Blair remained unconvinced. Otis settled on the floor beside Jean, allowing Blair to relax and attack her soup again.

"You know they've found Jimmy Boyd's body," Jean said.

"No, I didn't." Blair continued to eat her soup as if she'd heard nothing more important than the day's weather.

"Was Jimmy Andy's father?" Jean asked.

"I dunno, I suppose he could be." Blair tore off another piece of bread and began gnawing distractedly at it.

Jean stayed silent for a few minutes, Andy comfortable in her arms, Blair preoccupied with the soup and the baguette. Finally, Blair put down her spoon and looked up at Jean. "What?" The question sounded more like an admission of guilt.

"Is that supposed to be a question?"

"You're pissed at me."

"I'm wondering what your plans are, that's all," Jean said and then added, "Now that you're reunited with Andy."

That seemed to stump Blair. Then she delivered another one of the shrugs Jean was getting used to. "Find a nice place to live with Andy, I guess. Get a job."

"Are you still hungry?" asked Jean. "Do you want something else?"

"You wouldn't have any dessert, would you?"

"Got some apples in the fridge."

Blair made a face. "I mean something sweet."

"Sorry."

Jean handed Andy back to Blair and then sat across from her at the kitchen table. "Listen to me, Blair," she said, training a hard gaze on the young woman. "I don't want to scare you but Max Flagg is still out there. The police suspect him of Jimmy's murder but they don't have enough evidence. They've got him for something else, too, but right now he's out on bail and probably willing to do anything to keep it that way—including coming after you."

Jean's words had the effect of finally capturing Blair's elusive attention. She looked suddenly fearful. She didn't say anything, clutching Andy closer to her.

"Would you like me to suggest something?" Jean continued.

"I—I guess so," Blair stammered.

"Stay with me for the next while. Max is going to land in jail and land there soon. Meantime, he has no idea where you are and he doesn't know who I am. That means you're safe here. Out on the street, you're not so safe."

"You would do that for me?" Blair sounded as though she could not quite believe what she was hearing.

"I don't want anything to happen to Andy or to you," Jean said, thinking that if she were honest, it wasn't so much Blair she was concerned about as little Andy.

"I really appreciate you doing this," Blair said in a way that suggested she found it hard to admit her appreciation.

"Good, then it's settled," Jean said.

"Is there any more soup?" Blair asked.

Andy reached out, straining toward Jean. "He wants you to hold him," Blair said. She did not seem unhappy about it.

Jean took him in her arms. He gurgled in delight.

"He likes you better than me," Blair said.

"He just hasn't seen you for a while, that's all."

But secretly, Jean was pleased.

44

The continual ringing in his bandaged head reminded Max that the bitch who had clocked him had also stolen his Cadillac. She had taken his dog. She had broken into Dynamic Electric and stolen the photographs that were his leverage with Peter Earp.

As he sat uneasily at his desk, his head throbbing, his body aching, feeling like total shit, he tried to console himself. At least she had left the Cadillac in the lot, and as far as the dog was concerned, he never liked that goddamn dog, anyway, never much of a guard dog, a big goddamn baby.

His bigger problem was the cops. With this latest arrest, he was looking at real prison time given his track record and seeing as how they had found him with his head cut open on the floor of the goddamn house, he didn't have much of a defense.

The Toronto cops had gotten the Milton police involved and that sure as hell wasn't good. Everyone was piling on, believing he knew more than he was telling them. They didn't buy the notion that he just happened to break into that particular Bridal Path home. There was more to it, they said.

The suggestion was that if he owned up to what was behind the break-in, there might be a reduced sentence.

Well, he did know more than he was telling them.

A lot more.

He was pissed at goddamn Pierre Dorval for getting him into this mess in the first place, for not telling him whose house he was breaking into or what was on the flash drive he was supposed to retrieve. Peter goddamn Earp.

Then there was the problem of Burke Murdoch. Max was pretty confident, despite the pressure on him, that he wouldn't talk, not if Pierre took care of him. Burke, he wasn't so sure of. Not that he knew much, but maybe enough to get them into even deeper shit.

His cell phone began to vibrate in his pocket. Painfully, he struggled to get it out and swipe it open. "How are you doing?" Pierre Dorval asked.

"Thinking about you, asshole. Why the hell didn't you tell me it was Peter Earp's house?"

"It wasn't information you needed to know," Pierre replied.

"Except that as soon as I got in there, I knew."

"What I'm concerned about is what you told police."

"Didn't tell them shit," Max said.

"You're a standup guy, Max. I appreciate that."

"I'm a standup guy as long as things get taken care of."

"I'm working on that now," Pierre said.

"What the hell does that mean?"

"It means that as long as you stay calm and don't say things you're not supposed to, I'm going to get you out of this."

"That's good," Max said, somewhat relieved.

"What about your associate?"

"Burke's cool," Max said, making himself sound more convinced than he felt.

"I'll be in touch."

When Pierre hung up, Max limped outside feeling a whole lot better than he had a few minutes before. He lit a cigarette, inhaled deeply. Even better.

Standing in the afternoon sunshine, finally calmed a bit as the pickup truck pulled into the parking area and that dickhead of all dickheads, Denny Pike, got out. Denny wore torn jeans and a grease-stained T-shirt, a Toronto Blue Jays ball cap and, as usual, a spaced-out, stupid expression, with the emphasis on stupid.

"Hey, dude," Denny called as he stumbled towards Max.

"Hey," Max said, thinking the last thing he needed right now was this prick.

"You got something for me or what?"

"Nothing today, Denny."

Denny's narrow, unshaven face showed a mixture of confusion and desperation. "You're kidding me, right, dude? I mean, come on, I drove all the way over here."

"Things are a bit overheated," Max said. "For the time being, we're closed down. Unless you'd like us to install a set of attractive pot lights."

"Don't need pot lights, dude."

"Yeah, but what you want, I ain't got. Okay?"

"Shit, man. I thought I could rely on you."

"Not this week Denny."

"Shit, shit," Denny said. He kicked at the ground and threw up his hands. "To hell with you, then. I take my valuable business somewheres else."

"Come back in a couple of weeks. I may have something for you then."

"Yeah, well, I can't wait no two weeks," Denny said.

"Okay, okay. I'll see you around." Denny started away and then came to a stop and turned. "The dog," he said.

"Dog?"

"The German Shepherd. What happened to the German Shepherd you had around here?"

"Took off, man," Max said. "Disappeared."

"Then it *was* him I saw," Denny said.

"You saw Otis?"

"He was with some chick and her baby. Walking along the street. I thought it was him, but I wasn't sure."

"Otis was with a woman? What woman?"

"You know who it was? That chick who used to be a Mountie. It was on television and shit. They threw her out of the Force and she came back here. It was all over the news."

Max stared at Denny in disbelief. "And this was who you saw with my dog?"

"Her and a kid, yeah. I mean, I'm pretty sure it was her. I asked her, and she didn't say it wasn't."

45

The garden in the rear of Peter Earp's house was so quiet Jean could believe she was in a country glade far from the city. She and Peter sat in the shade of the lush vegetation but even so Jean could feel the heat of the afternoon sun.

She asked, "How are you doing?"

Peter, his arm in an elaborate sling, pale and thinner than she had seen him, shook his head, a pained expression on his face as he said, "She shot me three times. They had to put a plate in my arm; I still don't have much use of it and at times the pain is excruciating."

"You're lucky to be alive," Jean said.

"You're right about that. She tried to kill me."

"Why do you suppose she would want to kill you?"

"I don't know. Your guess is as good as mine. I'm denying I did anything wrong. My lawyers are keeping the cops at bay for now. But at some point, I'm probably going to face charges in Milton. On top of everything, any development projects I'm involved in out there are dead in the water. To answer your question, no, I'm not doing great. But thanks for asking."

"I'm sorry to hear it," Jean said, not feeling sorry for him at all, something Peter immediately picked up on. He gave her an ironic smile:

"You don't give a shit." He made a dismissive motion with his hand. "It's all right, no one else does either. It's a good thing I'm more than capable of feeling sorry for myself."

He stared off and the silence of the garden rose up around them. Then he seemed to remember he had company and turned a haunted gaze towards Jean. "But you wanted to see me."

"Maybe some good news." She drew the envelope from her purse. "If Max Flagg was giving you a difficult time, he won't be doing it any longer."

"How did you find them?"

"The better question is how did Max get hold of them?"

"That's something I don't want to talk about," Peter said.

Jean showed him the flash drive. "Could he have gotten them off the video you secretly shot the night you spent with the premier of Ontario and her assistant?"

Peter's eyes lit with surprise. "How did you manage that?"

"That's something I don't want to talk about," Jean said.

"Good god." Peter shook his head. "I'll need that flash drive and the photos."

"Better if I hang onto them. They're safer with me."

The sun had moved down enough so that Jean had to shift her chair to keep a place in the shade. Once she had done that, she leaned forward to face Peter. "Here's the thing. I have the flash drive and the photographs.

Max won't be bothering you and you won't be trying to blackmail Amy and the Red Queen."

"I wasn't blackmailing them." Peter didn't sound convincing.

"If you weren't, you were intending to."

"I was hoping to do things another way," Peter said in a feeble voice.

"By blackmailing Amar Bal and his sister."

'I was only trying to help her."

"Here is what I want you to do. I want you to do your best to ensure that the charges against Tamara Bal are either dropped or severely reduced so that she doesn't do jailtime."

"Can I do that?"

"You can try," Jean said.

More silence. Jean could almost hear the wheels turning in Peter's head. The slick developer who could always find the way out, discovering that, this time, there was no way out.

"You know what frightens me the most about all this? My father-in-law. Or my former father-in-law, if I'm being accurate."

"Johnny Fish," Jean said.

"For God's sake don't call him that to his face," Peter said.

"You're still involved with him?"

"More than you can possibly know," Peter replied. "He's not going to like what's happened. He's not going to like it at all."

"Go to the police," Jean said, rising to her feet with the envelope. "I can't protect you, but they can."

Peter took this in and then shrugged. "I don't want to scare you."

"Then don't," Jean said.

"But if Johnny Fish knows that you know, you could be in as much trouble as me."

"Go to the police, Peter," Jean said. She started away.

He called after her. "Ironic, isn't it?"

She turned back to him. "I'm sorry?"

"Everybody blackmailing everybody. Everyone is trying to hide the truth of themselves from everyone else. And now here you are, Jean, the slightly tarnished heroine of the story, blackmailing the blackmailers."

"I suppose that's one way of looking at it," Jean said.

"There's another flash drive," Peter went on. "I had the original and took some screen shots that Max got hold of. But there was another copy."

"Where is it?"

"Think about it," Peter said. "You're pretty smart, Jean. You shouldn't have too much trouble coming up with the answer."

———

Sal and Britney from their white delivery van watched Jean emerge from the house.

"Well, what do you know?" said Sal.

"Miss Natural Bitch," Britney said sullenly.

"She doesn't need a lot of makeup, I like that," Sal said.

"You like that." Britney practically spit out the words.

"Question is, what was she doing with Earp?" Sal asked.

"Who gives a shit?"

"Lack of knowledge," Sal said. "That's what gets you into trouble."

"You got the hots for her. Nothing to do with any effing knowledge."

"I don't like it," Sal said watching Jean get into her car. "Every time we turn around, this babe shows up. What's going on here?"

They watched as Jean drove off down the street.

"Okay, now what?" Britney demanded.

"We hang in there," Sal said. "We do what we're supposed to do."

46

It was nearly dark by the time Jean started down the block to her house. In the waning light, she caught a glimpse of a big dog passing on the sidewalk, realizing with a start it was Otis.

She pulled over to the curb and then hopped out calling, "Otis!"

He was halfway down the block. She called again and this time he turned, his ears pricking up. When he saw that it was Jean, he bounded back to her, panting excitedly as she petted him and rubbed his coat. "What are you doing out here, boy?" she asked the dog. "Why did she let you out? Or are you running away from home?"

She caressed his ears and that caused him to yelp and that's when she saw the blood. "What happened, boy? Did someone hit you?"

She boosted him into the back and then got tissues from the glove compartment and used them to dab at the blood. Part of his right ear was nicked and bleeding. It looked as though Otis had run away before his attacker could do too much damage to him.

So who was his attacker?

A cold fear played along her spine. She reached into the glove compartment, pulled out the Glock from beneath the box of tissues and laid it on the seat beside her.

Heart beating faster, she drove to within a block of her house and parked. Otis was stretched out in the back apparently exhausted. Jean decided to leave him where he was. She grabbed the Glock and shoved it in the waistband of her jeans before she got out.

It was probably nothing, she told herself. Blair had accidentally let the dog out and he had run down the street looking for Jean and somehow hurt his ear. Everything was all right. She was being paranoid.

But just in case...

Jean slipped around to the back trying to remember if the glass door to the deck had been left unlocked. She pulled the gun out of her waist and started across the lawn. She was climbing the three steps to the deck when the back door suddenly opened and Blair stumbled into view, sobbing, her tear-stained face filled with horror.

She started to speak but was cut off as Burke Murdoch appeared. A hard blow from behind sent Jean pitching forward onto the deck. She managed to twist around in time to glimpse Max's contorted face.

She tried to get up but Max dug his cowboy boot into her rib cage sending her sprawling back. She lost her focus on the world. She heard Max shouting, "Bitch! Goddamn bitch!" while he kicked her again and again.

Kicked her until everything evaporated into darkness.

47

John Pesce had built his dream house at the end of a peninsula jutting into Georgian Bay not far from Thornbury. A rambling structure of wood and glass built into the side of the rock face falling to a boat house and a big dock.

Peter Earp had been there a couple of times with his wife during construction. But, as he got out of his car, this was the first time he had seen the place in all its completed splendor. Lots of style and elegance on the lakeside, Peter thought, what you'd expect from a guy like John. He reached the main entrance and was about to knock when the door opened and John himself said, "Come on in, Peter."

Dressed in white slacks and a short-sleeved, navy-blue Ralph Lauren Polo shirt, John turned away to allow Peter to follow him inside. They crossed a great room that opened onto a deck affording the expected spectacular lakeview. Why would you build a place like this unless it had a view to take a visitor's breath away? Peter thought.

"It's beautiful, John," he said aloud.

"Yeah, I guess you haven't been here since it was finished."

"First time," Peter said.

"Brenda and I love it and it's great for the grandkids."

"I'll bet," Peter said.

"Can I get you something? I was just going to pour myself a beer."

Peter wasn't a beer guy, nonetheless he said, "Sure, that's fine."

"Go out to the deck, enjoy the view," John said. "I'll be back in a minute."

Peter stepped onto the deck to lean against the railing. He tried to relax. It was going to be all right. All he had to do was get through the afternoon.

The lake was like glass, not a boat or another human in sight. The region was a huge tourist attraction at this time of the year but for now he and John could be the only two people in the world.

John appeared with two long-necked bottles and handed one to Peter. "Local craft brewery that I support," John said. "They make an excellent lager."

Peter took a swing from his bottle and thought it tasted like any other beer. Nonetheless, he said to John, "Very good. Thanks."

"Cheers," John said, clanking his bottle against Peter's. He put his bottle down on the railing and said, "How are you feeling?"

"Sore," Peter said. "And my arm's screwed."

"Nothing the doctors can do?"

"It's out of the sling so that's good," Peter said. "They say I'll get some use of it back with lots of physio but I'm not so sure."

"Time will tell," John said non-committally.

"Yeah, I guess it will."

"Meanwhile, the Milton development is dead, I assume."

"Maybe not," Peter said. The look that crossed John's face made him immediately sorry he spoke quite so boldly.

"Maybe not?" John raised eyebrows. "You've got to be kidding."

"I realize there have been setbacks, John."

"Setbacks?" His former father-in-law looked as though he couldn't quite believe what he was hearing.

Peter had no choice but to plough ahead: "I acknowledge there have been problems, no doubt about it. But there is a deal to be made in Milton. I am determined to make it happen."

"Well, I admire your tenacity if nothing else, Peter. But tell me, why did you try to extort the mayor by giving his daughter ten thousand dollars?"

"That's the allegation they're making," Peter said. "It's not true, John. I swear to you."

"Look, I want to help you, Peter," John said. "That's why I asked you to drive up here today. But it's no good if you're going to lie to me. I'm not saying what you tried to do was necessarily a bad idea, I simply have to know what we're liable to encounter with the authorities going forward."

"I understand that," Peter said.

"Then tell me the truth."

"What makes you so sure I'm not telling the truth?" Peter failed to keep the annoyance out of his voice.

"Peter, please. Stop wasting my time. Let's get this behind us so we can move on together."

Peter let out a sigh, the release he probably needed right now, he thought. He took a deep breath before delivering the story that he concocted for the police. "Yes," he said. "It's true. I gave money to Tamara. We'd become lovers. I knew she had a gambling problem. I mean, if you met her, she's this innocent-looking thing, you'd never think she couldn't stay away from the roulette wheels at casinos around the province. A roulette wheel. Can you believe it?"

"Unbelievable," John said.

"She was in a panic, scared that her brother would find out what she had been doing. I floated her a loan, that's all. The next thing she's accusing me of trying to blackmail her brother. Crazy, don't you think?"

"You did give her the money, then."

"Yes, but like I said—"

"Sure, sure, I understand. You were trying to help."

"That's all it was, John. Swear to god. I do believe Tamara has emotional problems. That's why the gambling. That's probably why she shot me."

"Emotional problems, eh?"

"I can't think of another explanation for the way she behaved," Peter said. "She's receiving psychiatric help as we speak."

John gave the same fatherly smile with which he had blessed Peter in the first days after he married his daughter. It was not a smile he had seen for a long time and it had a comforting effect on him, the worst of the storm passing, although, to Peter's relief, it had not been much of a storm.

"Tell you what, Peter," John said. "Why don't you go in the kitchen and get us a couple of more beers? Then we can discuss next steps."

"Sure, John, good idea," Peter said. "Give me your bottle."

John handed over his empty bottle and Peter went through the glass doors into the great room and down a corridor leading to the kitchen. He didn't really want another beer, but this was no time to be anything but cooperative with his former father-in-law.

Play it cool and calm like you always do, he thought to himself. You're going to get through this. You're going to be all right. Nobody tried to blackmail anybody. It was the mayor's word against his, and the mayor was trying to protect his sister.

He started toward the refrigerator, seeing the blue plastic sheeting spread across the floor. Strange, he thought vaguely. Maybe the sink had leaked or something. But then why would you have to cover the entire floor with plastic?

He was startled to see a young man in a white T-shirt and jeans, seated at the kitchen table. "Hello," the young man said politely.

"Hey, you scared me," Peter said.

"Sorry about that," the young man said.

"Just getting a couple of beers."

The young man said, "They're in the fridge."

Peter started to the refrigerator. He had a moment to see a large blond woman out of the corner of his eye, a hammer raised in her hand.

The hammer smashed against Peter's skull. The force of the blow threw him against the refrigerator. The young woman grunted with the exertion of hitting him again and again, blood flying everywhere.

48

Jean dreamed of a better place.

No particular geographical location she could put her finger on, simply the better place that exists in dreams.

A dream. Only a dream.

She opened her eyes to the darkness of the real world. Not a dream, a nightmare.

And the pain that accompanied the nightmare. And the dreadful stench that choked her nostrils and filled her mouth, making it difficult to breathe. She tried to move, hit the metallic side of something. Terror as she realized she was entombed in a coffin-like structure.

Frantically, Jean kicked at the wall, accomplishing nothing more than a hurt foot. She used her shoulder to brace against what she now imagined was the door to her tomb. Hurled herself into it again and again.

Suddenly, there was a sucking sound and the door popped open and she spilled out, falling to the ground, sobbing for air. She found herself in a field, down on all fours. She rose a bit so that she could see around her. The battered white refrigerator that had been her prison leaned against an elm tree. A second refrigerator lay on its side behind the tree.

The field, flat and barren, running to an abandoned one-story stone farmhouse, black against a sun bleeding streaks of red and gold across a bleak land uneasily awaiting the developers' arrival.

Jean got to her feet, for the first time realizing that she was naked. She looked around for any sign of Blair and the baby. There was nothing. The wind whistled around her, gaining strength in the dying of the day.

She was in the middle of a farmer's field with no clothes on.

God! She thought.

Sounds came from a grove of trees to the right of the farmhouse. Someone was digging. From the exclamations of frustration on the wind, the diggers were not happy.

She became aware of another sound: desperate pounding from the refrigerator turned on its side. Jean hurried over, yanking at the handle. Again, there was a loud sucking sound as the door popped open, a putrid stink exploding into the air.

Blair lay naked, twisted in the bottom, mouth opening wide gulping for air. Jean eased the young woman out and onto the ground. She lay on her side, alternately sobbing and gasping for air.

In the nearby wood, the digging sounds ceased. It was almost dark, clouds beginning to obscure what was left of the sun. The wind had become stronger and it was growing colder.

"Blair," Jean said, "we've got to get out of here."

"Can't," Blair groaned. "Feel awful."

There was movement from the wood, through underbrush, headed towards them.

"They're coming back," Jean hissed. "Come on, let me help you up."

Jean pulled at Blair, finally yanking her to her feet. Sobbing, Blair slumped against Jean and then together they started across the field. Jean wasn't sure where they were headed. Away from this wide-open place, that much was certain. The farm house? Better than stumbling around out here naked.

Behind them, someone called out. Jean glanced back. Max and Burke were in view, shovels in their hands.

Spotting Jean with Blair, the two men dropped the shovels and started running towards them. Jean began running too, dragging the semi-conscious Blair with her. But it wasn't enough. Jean was too exhausted, in too much pain, and Blair was too much of a dead-weight to outrun their pursuers.

Max swooped down, coming abreast of Jean, shouting incoherently then clutching at Blair and flinging her down on the field. Jean stopped and Max slugged her, knocking her to the ground. In the last fading light of the sun, Max grabbed her hair, shouting at Burke, "Get the other one. Let's go!"

They yanked and dragged the two women back to where they had dropped their shovels, Jean struggling, crying out to Max to let her go. Max wasn't listening. "Not so tough without your baton, are you, bitch?" Max breathed.

Once they had regained possession of their shovels, the two men hauled the women into the woods, dragging them through scrubby brush into a clearing where two shallow graves had been dug. Max threw Jean down near one of the graves. Jean, covered in dirt, tried to sit up. Max knocked her back down. "Stay put, bitch," he said.

"Max, for God's sake, don't do this," Jean managed to say. Blair whimpered beside her as Burke forced her onto her knees. He had a gun and now so did Max.

"Max—"

"Shut your goddamn mouth!" Max shouted, his eyes wild, waving the gun. "I've had enough of your shit. *Enough!*"

"What are we doing, Max?" Burke, jittery, casting nervous glances in Max's direction. "What's happening?"

"What the hell do you think is happening?" Max was spitting out his words.

"Right now, all they're going to charge you with is a lousy burglary, Max." Jean spoke rapidly, the sentences tumbling out, jumbled together. "You shoot us and it's murder. The cops know what's been going down. You kill two women, Max. Think about it. They're going to know you two are responsible. You'll spend the rest of your life in prison. It's not worth it. Don't do this. Don't make it worse."

"Shut up!" Max screamed. His eyes had grown wilder.

"Jesus Christ, Max, maybe she's right," Burke said. His gun hand was shaking.

"She doesn't know shit!"

"Yes, I do, Max," Jean said. "I'm a former cop. Believe me, I know what the two of you are up against."

"I don't want to do this," Burke said. "It's too much. I don't want it!" Burke threw his gun down. "I'm getting the hell out of here."

"Don't be so goddamn stupid," Max yelled.

"Stupid? This whole thing is goddamn stupid." Burke started away.

"Get back here." Max's voice was high, breaking.

Burke stopped and turned. "I'm through with you. I'm out."

Max opened his mouth to say something and then apparently decided against it in favor of shooting Burke.

Burke stood still, a look of astonishment on his face. "What the fuck?"

"There," Max shrieked. "You satisfied? You happy?"

With Max momentarily distracted, Jean summoned what strength she had left and lunged at him, knocking him sideways. Meanwhile, Burke collapsed to the ground.

Max righted himself. Jean's attack appeared to have had the effect of calming him, allowing him to understand that what he had to do was not so much a matter of revenge but of survival. Jean saw his eyes settle and lose the wildness as he trained the gun on her.

A gunshot. Followed by a second gunshot.

Max's broad face went blank. He looked down at himself, at the two holes that had appeared at odd angles in his chest. He looked up to see Blair holding Burke's gun grasped in her hands just before she shot him a third time. The bullet went into his forehead before exploding out the back of his skull.

Max was dead before he hit the ground.

Blair, on her knees, trembling, dropped the gun. Her face, streaked with tears and grime, showed no emotion. Jean crawled over to her. "It's all right," she said. "It's over."

Nearby, Burke made groaning sounds and rolled on his side. Jean found Max's gun where he had dropped it and then kneeled to Burke.

He eyed her fearfully. "What are you going to do?"

"I'm going to put another bullet in you with Max's gun. You'll be dead and everyone will think Max killed you."

"Don't do that," he said in a feeble voice.

"Then tell me where Andy is. Tell me what you did with with the baby and then maybe I won't kill you."

"Kid's back at the house. He's okay. I wouldn't let Max touch him."

"What'd you do with our clothes?"

"Over there." Burke pointed a shaky finger in the direction of the gravesites.

Jean rose to her feet and went over to what were little more than shallow cavities. Their clothes were flattened at the bottom of one of the cavities. Jean shook out her jeans and T-shirt and got into them before helping Blair dress. Then she went back to Burke, still on his side. His face had become pasty, his breathing shallow. Blood seeped down his chest. "Gotta get me some help," he mumbled.

"Do you have a phone?" demanded Jean.

"In my pocket."

"I think we should walk away and let the piece of shit die," Blair said.

"No, please." Burke sounded more frightened than ever.

Blair started toward him. Jean missed the moment when Blair had regained possession of Burke's gun.

Jean stood in front of her. "Blair, give me the gun."

Blair hesitated. "We don't have to kill him. All we have to do is walk away. The rest will take care of itself."

"The gun," Jean said.

Blair shrugged and handed her the gun. Jean stuck it into her belt and then went back to Burke.

"Please," he said. "I'm goddamn dying."

Jean leaned over him, fished the cell phone from his pocket, and swiped it open.

49

A passerby had seen the big German Shepherd lying in a car and called police who arrived and smashed a side window in order to get the door open and rescue the dog. Apparently, he was happy to see officers. They reported they had never encountered such a friendly German Shepherd.

Neighbors reported hearing a baby's cries coming from Jean Whitlock's house. This was highly suspicious because as far as anyone in the neighborhood knew—and everyone thought they knew all about Jean—she didn't have a baby. More police were called. Responding officers found the rear door open and blood on the deck. Inside, they discovered a crying baby boy, approximately three months old. One of the female officers said as soon as she picked up the baby, he quieted and snuggled against her. She said she had never met such a happy baby.

When Jean arrived home, she discovered the broken car window and Otis missing along with baby Andy. Blair became hysterical, certain Max and Burke had kidnapped her baby and taken him god knows where. As events became clearer, the various crises began to resolve themselves.

Child Welfare returned Andy to his mother in fairly short order and the Halton Animal Protection gave up Otis after a lengthy interview during which Jean was finally able to convince officers that she was not evil incarnate for leaving the dog unattended in her car. Rather, she was a former RCMP officer kidnapped by thugs who *were* evil incarnate if only because of their treatment of Otis, never mind the humans they had almost killed.

Finally, the four were reunited, Blair cleaned up and looking relaxed as she changed a giggling Andy's diaper. Jean tried not to be jealous. Otis wagged his tail as he wolfed down his kibble, apparently happy to be back in what Jean hoped was now his home.

"Not that you have much choice, big guy," Jean said, ruffling the fur around the dog's ears.

And what of Jean herself?

What of me? Jean thought. Well, there were still a couple loose ends to tie up, weren't there? Better do it, she decided. What else was there at this point? Pet the dog. Tie up loose ends.

Stay alive.

In that order.

———

"The premier is anxious to speak with you," Amy Wu-Chan said when she finally returned Jean's phone call. "However, the premier prefers not to do it at her office."

"Where would the premier prefer to do it?" asked Jean.

"The premier is introducing a Canadian film to-morrow evening at the Bell Lightbox in downtown Toronto. Do you know where that is?"

"I know it," Jean said.

"She's already seen the film so she won't be staying. Why don't I meet you in the lobby and then you and the premier can talk as soon as she's finished her intro-duction."

"If that's the way she wants to do it," Jean said.

"In the meantime," Amy went on, "perhaps you can tell me what you intend to speak to the premier about."

"She wanted me to find out certain things."

"Yes?"

"I've found out certain things."

Amy said, "I'll be in the lobby waiting for you at eight-thirty."

———

The marbled lobby of the Bell Lightbox reminded Jean of the entrance to a high-end department store more than it did a temple to cinema. The movie gods of another era would have constructed a grand and gilded palace. The twenty-first century bean counters provided an escalator that did not take you up to ladies' fashions as might be expected but to the anonymous second floor. Amy Wu-Chan, resplendent in a shim-mering white pantsuit, gave her a perfunctory greeting. Amy then led her along a narrow corridor lined on either side with photographs memorializing Toronto film festivals past. She opened one of two doors and stepped aside so that Jean could enter a utilitarian conference room furnished with a long table and chrome-accented office chairs.

"Wait here," Amy said. "I'll bring the premier to you."

Amy shut the door before Jean could reply. She looked around before taking a seat halfway along the conference table. She sat staring into space, checking her watch from time to time. Twenty minutes passed before the door opened and Eve Harriot, wearing her trademark red blazer, strode in. Amy followed, closing the door while Eve shook Jean's hand and said, "It's good to see you again."

Jean wondered if it was.

"Let's sit down a minute," Eve said. "My feet are killing me. Do you hate wearing heels as much as I do?"

"Why I don't wear them anymore," Jean said.

"Lucky you," Eve said, plunking onto a chair and then easing out of what Jean suspected were flame-colored Christian Louboutin pumps. "That's better," she said, the relief showing on her face. She focused on Jean. "You've had quite a time lately."

"That's not how I would describe it," Jean said.

"Amy tells me that it is important that we talk."

"When we first met, you asked me to let you know if anything showed up in Jock's files that might be a problem for you."

"Did I say that?" The premier looked mildly surprised. "Have you found something?"

Jean withdrew the flash drive from her purse as well as the still photographs and laid them on the table. The Red Queen looked at them as though they might be radioactive.

"Okay," she said. "What am I to make of those?"

"Peter Earp intended to blackmail you with them."

Eve threw a glance at Amy. "Did you know about this?"

She was silent for a time. Finally, she said, "Peter never said anything about blackmail."

Eve used a manicured nail to tap at the photos. "What about these?"

"Taken from the video," Jean said.

"Have you looked at it?"

"I've seen it, yes."

"And?"

"And I think it has nothing to do with me."

Eve sat back with a heavy sigh. "It is good to get out of these shoes for a couple of minutes." She swiveled toward Amy. "Is there anything else tonight?"

Amy slipped beside the premier and then reached over to pluck the flash drives and photos off the table. "Nothing else this evening, Madam Premier," Amy answered.

The relief was tangible on Eve's face. Then her eyes turned back to Jean and she said, "You may not know this, but there is another flash drive."

"Yes," Jean said.

"I know this because Jock Whitlock before he died showed it to me and said he wouldn't make it public as long as I worked to approve Peter Earp's development plans for the Milton area."

The surprise registering on Jean's face caused the premier to smile knowingly. "Peter didn't have to blackmail me. He could get Jock to do it for him."

"I didn't know anything about this," Jean said.

"Why should you? Jock is dead but where was his copy of the video?"

"Which is why you talked to me," Jean interjected.

"Amazing, isn't it? One night of bad judgement caught on video. Everyone scared. Everyone using it as a weapon to get what everyone wants. Consenting adults having sex together. What's the big deal? But look at the trouble it's caused."

Jean didn't say anything.

The premier's gaze moved to the hovering Amy. "What did you think, Amy? Did you ever think you'd end up in politics like this?"

"There remains the problem of this other flash drive," Amy said.

"Can you help us?" The premier was back to Jean.

"I think so," Jean said.

"Okay, let's suppose you can," Eve said. "What's it going to cost me?"

"It's not going to cost you anything."

"Then you may be the only person in this province who doesn't want something from me."

"Maybe I am," Jean replied.

"You must want something out of all this."

"I've already got what I want," Jean said.

Eve looked vaguely surprised. "What's that?"
"A dog," Jean said.

50

The tiny gray-frame house sat around the corner from Milton's Town Hall. Acquiring it had allowed Grace Travis to walk to work each morning so she could devote more steadfast, loyal service to Mayor Jock Whitlock. Grace looked only mildly surprised when she opened the door to find Jean on the threshold.

"You should have called," Grace said. "I would have prepared something for lunch."

"Can I come in?"

"You're always welcome, Jean."

She stepped aside to allow Jean in and then led her into her pin-neat living room. "I must say you don't look any the worse for wear considering your adventures of late," Grace said. "Can I get you something? Coffee? Tea?"

"No, I'm fine thanks."

"Oh, dear, why do I suspect this is not a social call."

"I'm afraid not," Jean said.

"Then please, sit down. Let's have at it."

Let's have at it. Not a sentence Jean would have associated with Grace, the longtime keeper of the mayor's flame. And she did look abruptly rather formidable as she perched on the edge of an easy chair, body tense as though ready for a fight.

"The files that you sent over to me," Jean began.

"The files that were stolen."

"I don't think you sent everything. I believe you sent me a lot of stuff that you hoped would throw me off the track. You weren't expecting they would be stolen but you *were* expecting them to be harmless and they were."

"I didn't think there was anything to hide because the mayor at the end had nothing more to hide," Grace countered in a firm voice Jean previously would never have associated with her.

"Yes, but you're not telling me the truth, Grace."

"You keep saying that but I am," she asserted.

"You knew I would find the key to the storage locker and sure enough I did. Except there was nothing in there but the phony suicide note that you wrote."

"You keep repeating these untruths," Grace said testily. "What do you want from me, Jean?"

"There's probably more but all I want is the flash drive Jock left behind when he died."

Grace made a face. "I don't know what you're talking about."

"Yes, you do. Look, I know you're trying to protect what little of Jock's reputation there is left to protect. I don't want to do anything more to him than is necessary. I'm not going to do anything with that flash drive but destroy it and hope there aren't any more copies."

Grace became silent and then, just as Jean was certain she wasn't going to say anything, the air appeared to go out of her body. She shook her head as though forcing herself to focus before she said carefully, "All right. As long as you promise that's what you're going to do."

"We can destroy it together if that's what you'd like."

"No, I trust you, Jean. You've always been honest with me—unlike your uncle, I should say."

She rose from the chair and disappeared from the room, returning moments later with the flash drive gripped in her small fist. "There you go," she said, her voice clipped and angry. "I hope you're satisfied."

"There is something else," Jean said.

Grace looked perplexed. "What?"

"I'm not sure, but something that the people following me around wanted. They broke into my house twice, and knocked me out as I left Jock's storage unit. Those people were looking for something, Grace. The thing is they're not going to stop looking and that puts us both in danger. So. What is it?"

"You're imagining things." Grace's voice had grown small, the anger and authority draining out, replaced by uncertainty.

"No, I'm not, Grace."

For a time, she sat so still she might have turned to salt. But then, swiftly, she was on her feet, again charging from the room. For the next five minutes, Jean sat in silence, listening to the creaking sounds of the old gray house.

And then, as fast as she had disappeared, Grace was back with a notebook. She dropped it beside Jean. "There," she pronounced. "There it is." Tears sprang into her eyes. "You're going to read it and you're going to think what an awful person I am not to have shown anyone this earlier. I was trying to protect the man I loved so much. I thought it was better for him that it stays hidden. I don't know. Maybe I was wrong. Judge for yourself."

It was a black and white composition book, the kind that a student in grade school would use. Inside, the lined pages were filled with Jock Whitlock's handwriting, the cursive Jean immediately recognized as his.

Jean stood and Grace feinted toward her and for one wild moment, Jean thought the woman who loved Jock Whitlock more than anything might hit her. But instead she said, "Good night, Jean, and please, don't come back again. Ever."

51

Blair said she was still having trouble adjusting—things like taking care of a baby all day long. Would Jean mind babysitting Andy for the night so she could get some sleep? She hadn't been sleeping well lately, anyway. Nightmares about what had happened to her, about Jimmy Boyd's murder; nightmares about what was going to happen to her in the future.

Jean pretended to do it grudgingly, understanding Blair needed time to make certain adjustments. Secretly, she was delighted to have Andy for another night. As she settled into bed with Jock's notebook, Andy was in her arms, Otis sleeping peacefully pressed against her so that for the first time in a long time she felt warm and safe.

That feeling didn't last long. As she read through the notebook, Jean began to feel anything but warm and definitely not safe.

Jock, as she always suspected, had not died with a clean slate, all his secrets revealed. There were plenty more he had consigned to the notebook she held in her hands.

The secrets that got him killed.

At midnight, Jean phoned Mickey Dann. "Are you awake?" she asked when he answered.

"I am now," he said. "Don't tell me. You're calling to ask me out."

"That joke is getting old," Jean said.

"Is it?"

"However, as it happens, that's exactly what I'm doing," she said.

"You're kidding."

"What's open around here at this time of night?"

"You want to meet now?"

"You have something better to do?"

"How about sleeping."

"Sleep when you're dead. Meet me at Victoria Park in an hour."

"This is your idea of a date?"

"Are you going be there or not?"

"I must be crazy," he said.

"That makes two of us," she replied.

———

The unknown soldier stood endless guard outlined against the clear night sky. Victoria Park was eerily quiet, the hollow click of Jean's boot heels on the inlaid brick the only sound as she carried Andy in his car seat along the walkway.

Mickey was already there, a ghostly, unshaven figure in the light thrown off by a nearby streetlight. He wore an untucked shirt that needed ironing over baggy khakis Jean would have encouraged him not to wear. He sat on the same bench where for years she had lunched with Jock. Fitting, Jean thought to herself as she approached Mickey.

"You brought a baby along on a date?" Mickey asked. Andy smiled, happy at the prospect of a new distraction.

"Don't the women you date bring their children?" Jean asked, seating herself beside him, moving Andy out of the car seat onto her lap.

"The women I date don't have children," Mickey said.

"Maybe it's time you started dating women your own age."

"What about Blair Lalonde? Isn't she, like, his mother?"

"Blair is having a rough time," Jean said. "She needs sleep."

"So do I," Mickey said.

"Just be glad I didn't bring the dog," Jean said. "Reach into my bag, will you? There's a notebook I want you to take a look at."

Mickey picked up the bag and found the notebook while Jean held onto the baby. "What is this?" he asked.

"Just read it," Jean said.

He laid the notebook in his lap and opened it up. When he saw what was written on the first page, he looked sharply at Jean. "Is this what I think it is?"

"Read," Jean said. "And then we'll talk."

He leafed quickly through the pages, skimming some, reading others more closely. When he finished, he closed the notebook and said, "Jesus Christ."

Andy made smacking sounds as he slept on Jean's lap.

"This is Jock's handwriting," Mickey said.

"Yes, it is," Jean agreed.

"Where did you get it?"

"In a storage unit nobody knew anything about," Jean said. A white lie but it kept Grace out of it.

"I'll have to look at it more closely but I'd say this notebook answers a lot of questions about what Jock was up to and who he was up to it with," Mickey said.

"Not just Del Caulder," Jean said.

"Someone worse than Del," Mickey said. "And that's saying something."

"It also creates a lot more trouble," Jean said.

"We're going to need more than Jock's notebook."

"That's why I wanted to talk to you," Jean said. "I've got an idea how we can handle this."

"*We* are not going to handle anything," Mickey said.

Jean shook her head. "You turn that notebook over to the OPP and who knows what will happen to it."

"Then what?"

"My idea," Jean said. "If we do this right, no one can make that notebook go away."

"I hate this," Mickey said.

"Why?"

"Because it means I'm in more trouble than ever."

52

From its perch atop the Niagara Escarpment, the restaurant overlooked Hamilton's harbor and Lake Ontario. On a clear day, Jean mused as she drove into the parking lot, you might be able to see Buffalo. Otis stirred in the back seat as she came to a stop, rising expectantly to his haunches.

"Sorry, boy," Jean said to him. "I'm going to have to leave you here but I won't be long. Don't let anybody take you away this time, okay?"

Otis cocked his head as though trying to understand what she was saying. Jean couldn't blame him for being confused. These days, she operated in a constant state of confusion. No different this morning, she thought, as she rolled down her window halfway so that Otis would have air.

Hamilton under a blue sky sprawled around her as she emerged from the car, deceiving, hiding its industrial roots, the former Steel Town lurking somewhere beneath a green canopy of trees behind the towering glass and steel structures that partially obscured the view of the waterfront.

Vans were scattered around the parking lot. Two big industrial garbage bins flanked either side of the entrance. The door was propped open so Jean could enter.

The interior had been pretty much gutted, streaks of light seeping through a big grimy window turned swirling dust particles to gold. Lumber was piled among industrial wood saws. Plastic sheeting was hung on the walls. John Pesce sat at one of the dining tables left behind when the place was cleaned out. He was well-dressed, Jean noted as she approached, but his face was the color of chalk. He did not rise. Instead, he made a curious waving motion with his hand.

"When we're finished, this will be Hamilton's best Italian restaurant," he announced in a weak, gravelly voice, the voice of a sick man. The welcoming hand pointed at the window. "With a spectacular view."

"Just what the city needs, another Italian restaurant," Jean said dryly.

"We're trying to come up with a name. Got any suggestions?"

"How about, Another Damned Italian Restaurant?"

He gave a strained smile. "You know what? I kind of like it."

"Feel free to use it," Jean said. "It pretty much sums up my feelings about Italian restaurants."

"Sorry, I don't stand," he said. "I've just come from the Juravinski down the road. Kinda knocked me out this morning."

"That's the cancer center?"

"That's right," John said. "I'm a frequent visitor."

"Sorry to hear it," Jean said.

The welcoming hand waved dismissively. "Age," he croaked. "The doctors tell me everyone gets this in one form or another. You like to think you're that one guy. But then it turns out you're not. What can you do?"

He studied her with baleful eyes. "Why don't you sit down?"

She drew up a chair across the table from him.

He said, "I've been hearing a lot about you."

"I've heard a lot about you. John Pesce. Johnny Fish."

His chalky face darkened. "Nobody calls me that."

"They do. They just don't do it to your face."

He issued a burst of mirthless laughter. "But you do, huh? You're tougher than the rest, I suppose. At least that's what you like to think."

"I'm pretty tough, John. Tough enough to get here, to be with you today."

He studied her some more as though trying to gauge how much truth was in her words.

"You know my uncle," she said.

"Your uncle," he replied.

"Jock Whitlock."

"Yes, Mayor Jock Whitlock. I liked Jock. A good man."

"The good man you killed," Jean said.

———

Mickey Dann sat in his car, not far from where Jean had parked. He drummed his fingers against the steering wheel debating whether he should go inside. Angry with himself all over again for going along with Jean's so-called plan. If you called facing a dangerous old lion in his den—or in his under-construction Italian restaurant—a plan then he supposed he was part of a plan. A peripheral part, for sure, the supporting role, definitely.

Mickey sat for a few more minutes and then got out. He could see something moving around in Jean's vehicle and realized with a start it was the goddamn dog. What was she thinking bringing a dog to this particular party?

He walked to the car. Spotting him, the dog began barking and smashing himself against the side window, making an awful racket. The dog was going to screw up everything, Mickey thought. Believing he might quiet the animal, Mickey opened the back door. Immediately, the dog bolted out and shot across the parking lot out of sight.

Shit, Mickey thought.

53

John Pesce appeared unperturbed by Jean's accusation.

He merely said, "My understanding is that he committed suicide. Hanged himself from a lamppost."

"You arranged to make it look like that."

"Did I? And why would I do that?"

"I don't know, Johnny, why does anyone in your line of work want anyone dead?"

"You tell me," John replied.

Instead, she opened her shoulder bag and pulled out Jock's notebook and laid it on the table in front of him. "What's this?" John demanded. "Your homework?"

"Jock's handwritten journal," Jean said. "The reason why you killed him. The journal he must have told you about. The journal you've been trying to find. It's full of all sorts of accusations and revelations. In his last days, I must say, Jock was feeling sorry for himself—and angry with you."

"Why would he be angry at me?"

"You were refusing to pay him; by this time, given the murder charges, he was of no more value to you. He was facing an expensive trial and going broke. He needed money, your money. He told you about the notebook. He had nothing to lose; he would take it to the police unless you funded his defense."

"Jock could be a bastard, no doubt about it," John said.

"He could but you were even worse, the kind of bastard who will kill you if you cross him. Jock crossed you. You didn't like that so you made sure Jock never did it again and could no longer talk to anybody about anything."

"Makes sense, I suppose," John said with a shrug. "As much as anything makes sense these days."

"But you didn't have the notebook. You figured it must be in the records Jock left behind and I had those records."

"What about it, Jean? Are you wearing a wire?"

"I'm not wearing a wire," Jean asserted.

"Not that it makes much difference. If you listen to my doctors at Juravinski, I don't have much longer. Whatever happens, my attorneys can probably keep me out of prison for as long as it takes. I'm not too concerned."

"If you're going to die, then why bother killing anyone?"

"Call it tying up loose ends," John said. "An unwillingness to be taken advantage of." He looked thoughtful as though taking seriously the question of why one human being would kill another. "Or maybe I didn't know at the time that my string had just about run out. A variety of reasons, I suppose."

He grew silent again. Jean thought she could hear something from outside, wasn't sure, but wondered about Mickey. He was late making his entrance to arrest this bastard.

John was talking again. "I'm sorry," Jean said. "What did you say?"

"I said, you know what I'd like right now?"

"I have no idea," Jean said.

"A beer. A nice cold beer. Would you join me in a cold beer?"

"It's a little early for me.".

"Then do an old man a favor, will you? There's beer in the kitchen refrigerator. Lager. I like a lager. Would you mind getting it for me? I don't move around so easily after one of my visits to Juravinski."

"Sure John, I can do that for you," Jean said, thinking it would buy some time to allow Mickey to get in here.

"Kitchen's down that corridor over there," John said.

Jean crossed to a short hall that led to what soon would become the restaurant's kitchen area. A two-door, stainless-steel refrigerator was to her left as she entered. First, she noticed the plastic sheeting covering the floor. Then she saw the skinny guy with the knife. By that time, she had the police baton out, snapping it to its full length. The skinny guy with the knife looked alarmed. "I didn't know it was you."

He paused too long—big mistake—allowing Jean the instant she needed to whip the baton across the skinny guy's face. His nose exploded in blood, and he dropped the knife as he fell back on the plastic sheeting screaming blue murder.

But she didn't react fast enough. What felt like copper wire coiled around her neck and the woman who had lunged up behind her tightened the wire with ferocious force, shouting something about killing the bitch. Jean understood vaguely that she was the bitch to be killed.

Jean pushed back hard, forcing her assailant into the hallway. She dragged Jean with her. Jean hit her again, broke free and stumbled away, able to breathe again.

Her assailant, a huge blond woman, meanwhile lurched away toward the main part of the restaurant. Jean caught up to her, smashing her with the baton. The woman yelled something as she fell to the floor. Out of the corner of her eye, Jean caught a glimpse of John Pesce only now he was on his feet moving forward.

Johnny Fish with a gun in his hand.

Frozen in place, unable to take her eyes off the muzzle of John's gun, something blurred past. It took a moment for her to realize Otis had taken flight, in the air, slamming into John as his gun went off. The old man fell back to the floor, Otis snarling on top of him, John trying to fend off his snapping jaws.

"Otis," Jean called. "That's enough. Otis."

She grabbed the dog by the collar and dragged him away. John lay on the floor, bleeding from the neck and face where Otis had torn into him. Jean pulled the dog back across the room, knelt to him, taking him in her arms, feeling the excited throb of his heart. "It's all right, boy," she murmured. "It's over. No one is going to hurt us."

She stood as Mickey stumbled into view, maintaining the proper shooting stance, making his way through the dimness, trying to take in what he was seeing. The blond woman on the floor groaned.

"There's another guy in the kitchen with a knife," Jean said.

"Jesus Christ," was all he could say.

54

The skinny guy, known as Salvatore "Sal" Raspoli, after extensive police questioning, admitted that he and the big woman with the white blond hair, aka Britney Baker, made their living killing people.

A pretty darned good living, Sal insisted.

They had been paid by John Pesce to kill Jock Whitlock and make it appear a suicide; to disappear Peter Earp so that he would never be found again; and to simply murder Jean Whitlock.

They had followed Jock late one night to the house he was building. He had been drinking so it wasn't hard to take him down as he emerged from his SUV. Britney had strangled him to death with a length of cord that they later used for the hanging. That's what Britney liked to do, strangle her victims, get really close to them as they died.

It was Britney's idea to hang the body from the lamppost on Main Street and make it look like a spectacular suicide. She had driven Jock's SUV with the body stuffed in back to downtown Milton, Sal following.

Hanging a dead body in the middle of the night turned out to be more difficult than either of them figured. Sal was sure someone would come along and spot them. But no one did and finally it was done to Britney's satisfaction.

A hanging man on Main Street. A notable achievement in Sal's estimation.

For her part, Britney claimed she was merely the victim of Sal's schemes. She did not want to participate but Sal beat her and sexually abused her, forcing her into submission.

Under police questioning, she repeatedly burst into tears.

As police dealt with Britney and Sal, John Pesce, aka Johnny Fish, succumbed, not to injuries sustained by an attacking German Shepherd but to the cancer that had been eating away at him for years.

The inquest into Jock's death was a perfunctory affair there being little doubt now as to how he had met his end. The day after the inquest concluded, Jean met with Milton's acting mayor, Amar Bal. Amar had decided not to resign and had told Milton's weekly newspaper, *The Champion*, that he would run for mayor in the next municipal election.

The afternoon was cool and threatening rain but nonetheless Jean and Amar met in Victoria Park, sitting on the bench where she and Jock once lunched together.

"Right here, this bench?" Amar looked around as though he half expected Jock to show up.

"Ever since I was a kid," Jean said. "I would sit here with him and eat his tuna sandwiches."

"I do not think I've ever had a tuna sandwich," Amar said with a laugh.

"Well, if it's any consolation, I never touch them now. The thought of them makes me nauseous."

"I am so sorry, Jean."

"Jock was lost to me a long time ago. He betrayed everyone, even the niece who worshiped him."

"I believe I originally asked you for any help you could provide in order to root out corruption and influence in this town. You've done more than I ever could have imagined."

"I'm not certain I did much," Jean said.

"The bad people are gone," Amar said. "The crooked developers who would prey on this community. Now we can try to proceed with intelligent, well-thought-out development that is based on the needs of the people."

"I hope you're right, but I wonder," Jean said. "How is your sister?"

"The crown prosecutor has agreed to probation and a suspended sentence. I am relieved. But I fear it will be a long journey for Tamara to regain her confidence and sense of self-esteem."

"I'm glad to hear she's not going to prison," Jean said. "Prison is not a good place when it comes to regaining your self-esteem."

Amar rose to his feet. "What of you? What are your plans?"

"I'm afraid I'm back to wondering what to do with my life. I'm like Tamara, I feel I've lost something. I'm not sure what it is or how to get it back. I suppose the search goes on."

"You are a good person, Jean. I'm sure you will find the answers you are looking for."

Jean stood. "I'm hope so."

"I had better get back to the office and the business of being acting mayor. Did I tell you, Grace Travis has agreed to come back to work with me?"

"Then the business of the acting mayor is in good hands," Jean said.

"Good luck," Amar said.

Jean took his offered hand. "You, too, Mr. Mayor."

"*Acting* Mayor, Amar corrected.

Jean watched him disappear back inside the Town Hall and then started across the street. She stopped when a car pulled up beside her. Mickey Dann was behind the wheel. Jean reached the other side of the street and waited while Mickey parked.

"Almost like old times," Mickey said as he came to her, nodding in the direction of the park.

"Except Amar Bal doesn't know anything about tuna sandwiches. And he seems to be honest. The two things that set him apart from Jock."

"His sister is a lucky lady," Mickey said. "Mind you, it helps that the man she shot is now dead."

"How have you been?" Jean asked.

"Wondering how you are."

"You could phone and ask instead of stopping me in the street."

"Or you could call me," Mickey said.

"I did call you."

"To get me out of bed in the middle of the night."

"Thanks to me, you're the hero cop of the moment."

"But I still don't have a date."

"Well," Jean said. "You can fix that any time you want."

"Maybe I will," Mickey said.

"I'll be waiting," Jean said, walking away.

Shaking his head, Mickey watched her go along the street. He called after her. "I never know where I stand with you."

She gave him a wave and kept walking.

55

The sunlit streets of Old Milton were still.

Fast-growing Milton was growing fast somewhere else. Here, life continued to unfold leisurely, the myth intact of a lazy Ontario hamlet, its voice low and its streets deserted save for a few dog walkers following meekly after their determined little mutts.

It wasn't until she turned onto her street that there was noticeable activity: a green truck at the curb, an elderly woman in a flowered dress weighted down by a big garbage bag, following a young woman with a baby cradled in her arms.

Blair with baby Andy. Jean's stomach fell as she hurried forward.

When Blair saw Jean approaching, she stopped, blinking nervously. Otherwise, her expression stayed neutral. Andy's eyes, on the other hand, brightened, and he reached out to Jean. She said, "Blair, what's happening?"

"This is my aunt," Blair said, indicating the elderly woman in the process of heaving the garbage bag into the back of the truck.

"Hey there," she called, limping over to where Jean was with Blair. "I'm Sarah."

"Aunt Sarah's gonna take me in for a while," Blair said quietly.

In a bright voice Sarah said, "My husband and I are up in Georgetown. Retired up there. We'll get Blair settled and straightened around."

"Yes," Jean said in a choked voice. Andy made sounds as he reached out to her. "Do you mind if I hold him a minute?"

Sarah didn't look particularly happy and neither did Blair. But she passed the baby to Jean. Andy snuggled happily against her. Tears streamed down Jean's cheeks. Blair's mouth was set. Her expression remained steadfastly neutral.

"Will you come back for a visit?"

Blair nodded noncommittally. Jean kissed Andy on his forehead. He struggled happily against her. "Goodbye, little Andy," Jean managed, her voice even more choked. "Love you, sweetheart."

Andy tweaked her nose. Jean passed him back to Blair. Andy voiced his objections. But only momentarily.

Jean watched Blair get into the passenger side, holding Andy. She should put him in his car seat, Jean thought. She almost said something but then didn't.

Sarah struggled behind the wheel, started the truck. She gave Jean a cursory wave as she drove off. Blair stared straight ahead.

Jean went into the house, grown eerily quiet without Andy. She sat in the living room, heartbroken. Despite her determination not to, she broke into loud, echoing sobs.

As she sat weeping, she heard a noise. Otis padded into the room, his head bowed as he came to her. He looked into her eyes beseechingly and she had this curious sense that Otis understood the pain of the loss she was experiencing.

He settled his snout on her lap. She ruffled the fur around his ears.

Beginning to feel better.

Acknowledgements

Writing novels set in your own backyard can be fraught with dangerous possibilities. If you write something with, say, the French Riviera as your backdrop, which I have done, you are far enough away that the locals can't come after you waving pitchforks, furious at how you have portrayed them.

On the other hand, a stroll along the tree-lined streets you write about in the community where you live, well, the townsfolk could just as easily grab you and hustle you off to hang from one of those Main Street lampposts where the fictional Milton mayor meets his end.

So far, I'm relieved to say, everyone in Milton has remained sanguine about the way their town is portrayed.

First of all, then, the author is thankful to a citizenry that has yet to rise up against him.

Next, I'd like to thank Rebecca Hunter, the director of Milton's J. Scott Early Funeral Home who has been a tireless supporter and sharp-eyed reader from the beginning. She even went along with me burning down her house in a previous novel.

My great friend Kim Hunter of Toronto's Humphrey Funeral Home, provided valuable advice and direction when it came to dead bodies and the ways in which they are investigated.

Jennifer Smith, who brilliantly designs the covers for these novels, is a friend and Milton community treasure.

What a pleasure it is to work with her and repeatedly take advantage of her enormous talent. Also, thanks to Adam Smith for arriving in the nick of time to take the photograph that only makes the cover look so much better.

Alexandra Lenhoff has been editing my books on and off since the 1990s. She returned to diligently work on this book and it is a delight to have her back.

Speaking of longtime editors, Ray Bennett of London, England, has been saving my rear end, editorially speaking, since the days when we toiled together at the Windsor Star. He was particularly helpful this time, his ability to tweak a sentence made Main Street, Milton a much better novel than it was before he got his hands on it.

Also, another longtime friend and frequent editor, David Kendall, got off a plane from New Zealand and almost immediately went to work on the galleys, thankfully once more joining in the difficult business of making the author look a darned sight better than he otherwise would.

As usual, many thanks to my brother Ric who manages the production details involved in publishing these novels. As I constantly say, and it remains true, I could not do any of this without him.

Finally, and most importantly, my wife Kathy who not only serves as invaluable first reader and supporter, but daily keeps me laughing and loving, reminding me how special life is with her.

She has promised to man the barricades should the mob show up waving pitchforks.

Mystery! Murder Milton!

Ron Base's Milton Mysteries

The Escarpment

Disgraced Royal Canadian Mounted Police officer Jean Whitlock returns home to Milton to care for her dying mother. Milton is the town west of Toronto where she grew up—the town she tried to escape so long ago. Now she is back, staying with her younger brother, Bryce, who runs the family funeral business. An early morning phone call brings them up to the escarpment to pick up the body of a young woman.

Who is the woman? Was she murdered? Or did she jump from the top of the escarpment? Halton Police detective Mickey Dann, who dated Jean in high school, would like to know. So would Jean's uncle, Jock Whitlock, the town's savvy, manipulative mayor, and Del Caulder, the ruthless, larger-than-life local developer determined to build luxury homes atop the escarpment.

Jean, haunted by her own demons, finds herself drawn into the mystery of the woman's death. She unearths long-buried secrets, not only in her own life, but the town's as well. Powerful local forces are working against her. Jean's life is in danger. In a town full of shadows and lies, nothing is as it seems.

The Mill Pond

Disgraced former Royal Canadian Mounted Police Corporal Jean Whitlock has returned to her hometown of Milton, Ontario, to try to pull her life back together.

It's not working out very well.

There is a body in the Mill Pond that Jean knows far too much about. The obsessed Mountie sergeant who tried to rape her in Afghanistan and then left her for dead, has shown up in Milton, once again threatening her life.

Before she knows it, Jean is entangled in a dark web of blackmail, murder, local corruption, and a far-reaching criminal conspiracy. She must learn all over again that the peaceful small town where she grew up isn't so peaceful anymore.

ronbase.com
ronbase@ronbase.com

Made in the USA
Monee, IL
19 May 2020